UNCOMMON CHAMPIONS

UNCOMMON CHAMPIONS

Fifteen Athletes Who Battled Back

by Marty Kaminsky

BOYDS MILLS PRESS
HONESDALE, PENNSYLVANIA

Boyds Mills Press, Inc.
815 Church Street
Honesdale, Pennsylvania 18431
Printed in the United States

Photo Credits:
P. 17: Erik Weihenmayer; p. 44: Claus Andersen/Sporting Image; p. 71: Nuveen Tour, Champions of Tennis; p. 81: Greg LeMond; p. 89: Diana Golden Brosnihan; p. 96: Bill Smith; p. 106: Advantage International; p. 141: Fitness Management.

The Library of Congress has cataloged the hardcover edition of this book as follows:

Library of Congress Cataloging-in-Publication Data

Kaminsky, Marty.
Uncommon champions: fifteen athletes who battled back / Marty Kaminsky.
—1st ed.
[152] p. : ill. ; cm.
Summary: Inspiring true stories of athletes who struggled with physical and mental adversity.
ISBN 1-56397-787-7
1. Athletes—United States—Biography. 2. Physically handicapped—United States —Biography. I. Title.
796/.087/0922 [B] —21 2000 AC CIP
99-68100
Paperback ISBN 978-1-59078-005-3

First edition
First Boyds Mills Press paperback edition
Book designed by David Justice
The text of this book is set in 13-point Sabon.

10 9 8 7

For my father, who has never flinched in the face of adversity: a survivor with a smile on his face and a story to tell; my writing mentor, Beth Levine, who has taught me to find lessons in daily life and then tell them in my own way; to my wife, Martha, whose limitless love, support, and good humor have provided the foundation from which I have built my life; and to my children, Leah and David, and the many children I have taught through the years, who are the reason I write anything at all.

Contents

Foreword by Bobby Valentine	5
Introduction	7
Erik Weihenmayer: **Seeing Things His Own Way**	10
Michelle Akers: **The Fire Within**	19
Ruben Gonzalez: **Street Survivor**	27
Gail Devers: **A Sprinter's Close Call**	35
Jim Eisenreich: **This Is Who I Am**	45
John Lucas: **One on One**	53
Mansour Bahrami: **For the Love of the Game**	64
Greg LeMond: **Making a New Plan**	73
Diana Golden Brosnihan: **Gliding on the Edge**	82
Chris Zorich: **Zora's Gift**	90
Zina Garrison: **No One Is Perfect**	99
Bob Welch: **Living One Day at a Time**	109
Willie O'Ree: **Breaking the Barriers**	117
Dan O'Brien: **No Sure Thing**	124
Jean Driscoll: **Don't Look Back**	133
Index	142

FOREWORD

by Bobby Valentine

Life has a funny way of throwing people some nasty curve balls. When I graduated from high school and signed with the Los Angeles Dodgers, I thought I was bound to be a big-time, big-league shortstop. But in the offseason, while I was playing intramural football at Arizona State University, I blew out my knee. Then two years later I was playing the outfield and I leaped to make a catch against the fence. My leg caught on the chain-link fence and was broken in two places. It never healed right, and though I played five more years in the majors, I just wasn't the same.

Baseball was my whole world, but at age twenty-nine I had to retire as a player because I could not run and field like I once could. Sooner or later everyone has times like these, when the disappointment and disillusionment feel like they might swallow you up. A part of you wants to give up and run in the other direction, but I have found that the best strategy is to face hard times head-on. I stuck with it: I became a minor-league instructor and then a third-base coach for the New York Mets in 1983. Soon after that I was managing the Texas Rangers, and eventually I returned to the Mets as their manager.

Over the years I have had my share of ups and downs, but each low time has helped me learn a lot about myself. Life is not always like sports, but the lessons I learned on the baseball and football fields helped guide me through the toughest times. We would all like a nice, smooth ride, but—like the Mets thrilling season in 1999—more often than not life is a roller coaster ride.

The stories in this book are about men and women who faced hard times and made hard decisions. These real stories about real people were an inspiration to me, and I know they will inspire you, too.

INTRODUCTION

She is curled in the starting blocks like a cheetah ready to pounce: head up, face drawn tight, eyes staring straight ahead. There is no time for thought; there is only time to run. At the crack of the starter's pistol she shoots out of the blocks, blazing ahead, legs and arms a blur. She kicks her knees high as she sprints, every muscle taut, every cell straining forward, ever forward. In the end she is one of three sprinters to power past the pack and burst to the finish line. With a final surge she lunges forward, her neck and head pulling her body across. In a split second it is over and Gail Devers has won again. She proved herself in 1992 and now again at the 1996 Summer Olympic Games, Gail Devers is the fastest woman in the world.

From the comfort of our television-room couch, my eleven-year-old daughter, Leah, and I watch the drama of these 1996 Olympics unfold. We sit mesmerized, watching Ms. Devers glide around the track, waving to the crowd, taking a final victory lap. Leah turns to me and says, "She makes it look so easy." And I have to admit that despite the obvious strain and sweat, the athletes on our television screen, like Gail Devers, do make it seem effortless.

Day after day, game after game, they throw, run, kick, and shoot baskets with an ease that I wish was mine. I remember watching the heroes of my own childhood, Sandy Koufax and Mickey Mantle, and thinking the same thing: they make it look so easy. As a boy I did not realize that the people on my television screen sometimes faced difficult decisions and hard times. Before winning her first Olympic gold medal in 1992, Gail Devers spent three years battling a severe thyroid condition that nearly claimed her life. She lay in agony on a hospital bed as doctors debated whether to amputate her leg to try and save her. Watching her, smiling as she salutes the crowd, it is easy to forget that she is not some athletic goddess; she is mortal like us, with many of the same joys and sorrows.

In fact, all of us sometimes confront situations that have no easy answers. These situations, when fortune or fate seem to turn against us, are known as adversity. On occasion the adversity is as small as a failed test or a broken finger. At other times adversity may loom as large as the catastrophic illnesses that threatened the life of skier Diana Golden Brosnihan. (She died in 2001, after this account was written.) None of us seeks out or welcomes adversity, but learning to deal with life's troubles shapes who we are.

This book contains the stories of fifteen remarkable people. They are remarkable not just for their achievements on the playing fields, courts, and tracks, but for the tremendous courage they demonstrated while overcoming major obstacles in their lives. Like you and me, they were sometimes embarrassed and ashamed of the problems that burdened them. "Why does this have to happen to me?" they asked. On occasion they tried to bury their problems, to run from them or wish them away, but eventually they realized that adversity can only be overcome by facing it head-on.

By looking in the mirror and admitting to a problem, by asking for help and by learning to find the strength within to face tough times, these athletes learned important lessons. It took courage, strength and determination for Dan O'Brien, Michelle Akers, and Erik Weihenmayer to pick themselves up and try again. It may look easy when they float over the pole-vault bar, head the ball past the goalie, or stand atop the mountain, but it is never easy to battle adversity when you are trying to realize your dreams.

I hope that these stories will remain in your heart so that when it feels like the odds are stacked against you, you will draw the courage, strength, and determination you need to make the right decisions.

Marty Kaminsky

Erik Weihenmayer

Seeing Things His Own Way

Erik Weihenmayer thrust his ice ax into the deep snow, hoping to grip a hold long enough to catch his breath. The howling winds, gusting up to 100 miles per hour, roared like a fleet of jet planes. To communicate with his climbing partners, Erik had to scream to be heard. It was only 3,000 more feet to the summit, but Erik's team was hopelessly trapped for five days in a blizzard on the high slopes of Mt. McKinley.

At 20,320 feet, Alaska's Mt. McKinley is the highest peak in North America. Freezing temperatures, sudden avalanches, and devastating storms make it one of the most difficult mountains in the world to climb. Nearly one hundred climbers have lost their lives there after falling into deep crevasses or being blown off the face by gale-force winds. For even the most experienced mountaineers and rugged explorers, climbing McKinley is the challenge of a lifetime.

Imagine climbing such a treacherous peak without being able to see a single step. That is the task that Erik Weihenmayer faced in June 1995. Erik is completely blind, having lost his vision at age thirteen due to a condition he was born with called retinoschisis. But blindness has never stopped him from living an exciting life and pursuing adventures most of us only dream about.

"I am not a daredevil," Erik explains. "I have a healthy fear and respect of the mountains, but I believe with proper training and skill a blind person can tackle some awesome challenges."

From a young age, life itself proved to be a challenge for Erik. When he was a three-month-old baby, Erik's eyes began to quiver and shake. His parents were alarmed and brought him to teams of specialists over a year and a half. The doctors diagnosed his problem as retinoschisis, a rare condition that causes pressure to build in the retina until it disintegrates, eventually leading to blindness. To view something directly in front of him Erik would have to look up, down, or sideways. He relied on his peripheral (side) vision to navigate his neighborhood and to do daily chores and tasks.

But Erik hated to be treated differently, so he learned to compensate for his poor vision. When he played basketball with friends, they helped him cover the court by playing zone defenses. They also learned to feed him the ball with a bounce pass. "Erik could hear a bounce pass," his father, Ed Weihenmayer, explains. "But lots of passes hit him in the face anyway. After most games Erik had a bloody nose and looked as if he was playing football, not basketball."

With the help of family and friends, Erik was encouraged to find creative ways to participate in everyday activities. When his brothers raced their mountain bikes over a ramp, Erik joined in, but sometimes he rode off the edge, picking up scraped knees for his efforts. Though he rarely complained or showed his frustration, Erik's family was aware of his struggles. His father solved the bike problem by painting the ramp bright orange. After two more months of bike stunts on the ramp, however, Erik's eyesight had deteriorated to the point that the ramp became an orange blur. He rode off his driveway one day and broke his arm.

Despite his failing vision Erik continued his attempts to blend in and be like everyone else. Frequently he walked into trees or doors, and he had constant bruises and black-and-blue shins. "I guess it was a lack of maturity on my part," Erik admits. "It was a sense of denial. I refused to learn to read Braille or to use a cane, even though I needed one for my own safety."

By the time he was thirteen, Erik's eyesight was completely gone. At first he tried to function without the use of canes or visual aids, but that proved dangerous. While visiting his grandparents, he stepped off a dock and fell eight feet into a boat. Though unharmed by the incident, it shook him up. Out of sheer desperation, Erik came to accept his blindness.

"I realized that if I got good at using the systems for the blind I would blend in better and be more like everyone else," he says. "If I didn't use my cane I would be stumbling about, and that would make me stand out more."

At fifteen Erik joined his high school's wrestling team. Because the sport depends on physical contact, strength, and instinct, Erik found he could compete on even terms with his opponents. He did not win a match as a freshman, but by his senior year he was chosen team captain and sported a 30-3-3 record. He was selected to represent Connecticut in the National Freestyle Wrestling Championships and went on to wrestle at Boston College.

Just as Erik was beginning to accept his blindness and learning to function in a sightless world, tragedy struck hard. While he was away at summer wrestling camp, Erik's mother was killed in an automobile accident. The loss was devastating, but Erik's father exerted extra efforts to spend more time with his children. As a way to bring the family closer, Ed Weihenmayer brought his children together for adventurous treks around the world. Among many other journeys, they visited the Batura Glacier in Pakistan and the Inca ruins at Machu Picchu in Peru.

"Facing his mother's death and blindness so close together was difficult," Ed recalls. "But Erik never used them as an excuse for not measuring up and going for it." Rock-climbing trips to New Hampshire and other travels with his family whet Erik's appetite for adventure. He soon became a skillful rock climber, scuba diver, and sky diver.

After graduating from Lesley College in Massachusetts, Erik was hired to teach at an elementary school in Phoenix, Arizona. Managing a class of lively fifth graders was a challenge equal to any Erik had undertaken, but he loved his work and handled it well. "My dad worked on Wall Street for thirty years," he says. "He struggled to find meaning in his work. I don't have that struggle as a teacher." The students in his classes quickly realize that Erik needs their help to make learning work for them. With his guidance they devise systems to communicate and get things done. Students pitch in taking turns writing on the board, hanging posters, and passing out papers. Although the class could take advantage of their sightless teacher, they rarely do. In fact, they fall over each other to be the first to fill his dog's water bowl.

As he settled into his teaching job, Erik and a buddy filled their weekends with climbing trips to the rock faces and mountains of Arizona. On the higher slopes Erik and his partners devised a climbing language that the lead climber would call out. If a teammate shouted, "Iceberg ahead," for example, Erik understood that a pointy rock sticking out of the ground was in his path. A cry of "ankle breaker" meant that little loose rocks lay ahead. By learning to follow in the footsteps of his partners and to rely on his other senses, Erik took on the tallest peaks in Africa and North and South America with his climbing friends.

"Feeling the rock under my hand, feeling the wind and sensing I am hundreds of feet above tree line is an incredible experience," Erik says. "It's exciting to work on a team for a common goal." So great is his love of the mountains that Erik and his wife, Ellen, were wed at a rock altar 13,000 feet up the slopes of Mt. Kilimanjaro in Tanzania.

But pulling yourself up a sheer rock wall, balancing on an icy ridge, and handling sub-zero temperatures can prove frustrating for any mountaineer, particularly one who is blind. While climbing Mt. Rainier in 1985 Erik discovered he could not set up his tent in the freezing weather with his bulky gloves covering his hands. In typical fashion he refused to admit failure. "I was so embarrassed that I resolved never to let that happen again," he says. "When I returned to Phoenix I practiced setting up a tent in the one-hundred-degree heat with gloves on over and over. It is no longer a problem for me."

Careful planning and practice have always helped Erik work around the problems caused by his lack of vision. To prepare for the risky climb up Mt. McKinley,

Erik's team practiced on Mt. Rainier in Washington and Long's Peak in Colorado. Back in Phoenix, Erik and a teammate strapped on fifty-pound packs and raced up and down the stairs of a forty-story skyscraper to build strength and endurance.

Before the McKinley trip Erik's climbing group, which called itself Team High Sights, secured the sponsorship of the American Foundation for the Blind. "I was hopeful that my climb would make a statement," Erik says. "Blind people have the potential to be productive members of society. With the proper support systems, preparation, and a resourceful mind, a blind person can lead a fulfilling life and compete in a sighted world."

Huddling in their ice-coated tents at 17,000 feet, Team High Sights was forced to wait out a five-day storm on Mt. McKinley. Their food supply was dwindling and all that could be seen of the summit was a plume of snow blowing hundreds of feet into the air. Unless the storm let up, all hope of reaching the summit would have to be abandoned. On the sixth day they heard on their weather radio the news they'd been waiting for: There would be a twelve-hour period of clear weather in which to reach the summit and return before the next storm system closed off the mountain.

Strapping on their ice shoes and insulated gear, the climbers tied themselves together with sturdy rope. Pushing through thigh-deep snow was exhausting

Erik Weihenmayer

work, but Team High Sights carefully moved up the mountain. For Erik, the climb to the summit seemed endless. At the top of a knife-edge ridge his ski pole slipped and all he could feel was air. "I was concentrating very hard with each step," he explains. "Finally I took a step and my friend Stacey said, 'Congratulations, you're on the top of North America.'"

With tears in their eyes, the climbers embraced and snapped photographs of each other. Erik held aloft a pair of banners—one designed by a girl at his school, and one for the American Foundation for the Blind. After fifteen minutes at the peak, the team headed down, safely making their way back to a lower camp.

The climb to the top of Mt. McKinley was a proud accomplishment for Erik, and one that he hopes provides inspiration for others. "Before McKinley I never thought I was extremely tough," Erik says. "I always felt I had the potential to do much more. As a blind person it is easy to sit back and allow others to do things for you. I hope my climb proves that we can all push beyond what we think we can do."

Having climbed McKinley, the highest mountain in North America, Erik is well on the way to meeting one of his climbing goals. In the next few years he plans to summit the highest peak on each continent, including Mt. Everest in Asia. He has learned to step around every obstacle in his path, and though it will be a difficult task, Erik knows there is no reason a blind man cannot sit atop the tallest mountain in the world.

Michelle Akers
The Fire Within

Michelle Akers lies flat on a stretcher in the locker room of the U.S. women's soccer team. An oxygen mask covers her nose and face. Two liters of intravenous fluid drip into her arms. She can barely make sense of the World Cup soccer game that is proceeding without her on the overhead television screen. Just minutes before, Michelle had been racing up and down the field, diving for loose balls and crashing between defenders to clear a pass. As regulation time wound down, Michelle lifted high in the air to deflect a shot and protect the scoreless tie with the Chinese team. She collided with U.S. goalkeeper Briana Scurry and dropped to the turf in a heap. Surrounded by team trainers, she walked away from the action wobbly-legged and confused.

Out on the field teammate Brandi Chastain lines up the kick that can bring the World Cup trophy to the United States. In the locker room Michelle joins 40 million American television viewers by sitting up to watch. When Brandi's blast settles into the net, the

Rose Bowl crowd of more than ninety thousand erupts and the U.S. women mob each other. Michelle rips the I.V. tubes from her arms, pulls off the oxygen mask, and summons up the strength to join her team in celebration.

Today is not the first time Michelle has staggered off a soccer field dizzy and nauseated. Since the start of the women's national team in 1985 Michelle has been its most dominant player but has suffered through several concussions, thirteen knee operations, and a nine-year battle with chronic fatigue syndrome that would have ended the career of most players.

The U.S. women's team came of age in 1999, but without the efforts of Michelle Akers, their oldest player, they would not sit atop the mountain. It was Michelle who scored the first-ever goal in team history in 1985. For more than a decade she was considered a powerful scoring machine much the way Mark McGwire is a big bopper in baseball. The bigger the game, the more likely it was that Michelle would drill home a goal or two, if not three. During the 1991 World Cup games she led all nations in scoring with ten goals in only six games. Before chronic fatigue slowed her pace, Michelle slammed in nearly a goal a game, an unheard-of average in the soccer world.

Tony DiCicco, coach of the 1999 World Cup team, describes Michelle as "the best soccer player ever to play the game; a woman among girls. In addition to incredible strength, speed, agility, acceleration, and size, Michelle's game is as solid as the Rock of Gibraltar. Her intensity for the game is what sets her apart. She goes all-out at all times and that sets an example for her teammates. When Michelle sets goals for herself, she is like a smoldering fire that burns through any obstacle in her way."

Most athletes take on a competitive attitude after years of games and competitions, but Michelle was a scrappy fighter almost from her birth. She was born in Redwood City, California, and lived there until her family moved to Seattle when she was in fourth grade. An energetic little girl, she played any sport that included a ball.

"If you gave her a doll she would throw it against the door," recalls her father, Bob. "But give her a ball and she would play for hours. She has always had great athletic skills and has always been stubborn and determined. Right or wrong, she won't back down."

When her family moved to Seattle, Michelle joined a soccer league sponsored by the police. At first she played goalie because that was where the best player was placed. When her coaches realized that she would steamroll over defenders to get a shot on goal, they moved her to the striker position so she could score. And score she did! In high school she scored at an astounding rate, often using her 5-foot-10 height to leap over defenders and head balls into the net. At the

University of Central Florida, Michelle was a four-time college All-American. When the first women's national team was formed in 1985, the decision to invite Michelle to try out was an easy one.

From the mid-1980s to the mid-1990s Michelle was widely considered the world's best player in the women's game. Her play in the 1991 World Cup final against Norway typifies her career. With the score tied 1-1 with less than three minutes to play, Michelle chased down a long pass near the Norwegians' goal. A defender reached the ball first and kicked it back to Norway's goalkeeper. Michelle pushed past two defenders and intercepted the pass before it reached the goalie. As the goalie frantically rushed to the ball, Michelle stroked it cleanly past her and into the left side of the net for the game-winning score.

When Michelle's teammates nicknamed her Mufasa after the lead character in *The Lion King*, they did so because of her long mane of hair and the tremendous strength she displays, both physical and mental. Since 1991, when she first contracted chronic fatigue syndrome, Michelle has relied on mental toughness, determination, and a strong Christian faith to pull her through hard times. Soon after the U.S. team won its first World Cup in 1991, Michelle started to experience symptoms of her illness. She was constantly exhausted and plagued by migraine headaches that sent her reeling to bed. For days on end Michelle stumbled around in a fog, dizzy, unable to digest her food, weary from lack of sleep, and weak from night fevers.

"I would lie there and wish I could die," she says. "I remember thinking that I would rather be dead than have to go through another day or hour like this."

She spent many hours crying in frustration and praying that the torment would soon end. At first her doctor told Michelle she suffered from mononucleosis and that a month of rest would provide the cure. After four weeks of bone-weary fatigue, however, she was rediagnosed as having the Epstein-Barr virus, which would require at least three months off the training field.

The confusing symptoms of the illness made it difficult to diagnose, but the final determination was that Michelle had chronic fatigue syndrome, a condition that can last anywhere from six months to a lifetime. According to the Centers for Disease Control and Prevention, CFS is "a disorder characterized by profound fatigue that is not improved by bed rest and may be worsened by physical or mental activity. Persons with CFS must often function at a substantially lower level of activity than they were capable of before the onset of illness." At least four hundred thousand Americans, mostly adults, are afflicted with CFS, and the symptoms may suddenly vanish or return at any time.

"During the worst period, which was probably the year and a half before the [1996] Olympics, there was not one moment's respite," Michelle told a reporter for *People's Weekly.* "It was just my mental tenacity that kept me going. I made myself get out of bed, made myself do things until my body just collapsed. And then I would go home and literally lie on the floor in my kitchen, because the floor felt cool, and just sleep there."

Michelle has described her battle with CFS as a twenty-four hour flu that will not go away. She continued to train and play soccer as best she could during this time, but it was difficult to perform when her balance problems and short-term memory caused her to forget where she was and what she was doing. On many occasions she called in sick because she could not find the energy to shower or brush her teeth, let alone to race across the field to track down a pass.

As weak as she was, Michelle still wanted to be on the field when the team competed in important games. Michelle bargained with Coach DiCicco to play as many minutes as possible. Some days she felt strong and could play an entire game, but more often she had to settle for playing a half and then receiving two liters of intravenous fluid to replace the minerals and liquids she lost.

To better preserve her energy the coaches moved Michelle to midfield so she did not have to run as much. Whenever possible she jogged instead of sprinting to cover her position. Because she was accustomed to running full speed for ninety minutes, these changes proved difficult for Michelle. "Nothing I had relied on in the past was there for me anymore," she explains. "My strength, stamina, energy, and self reliance—all gone. This illness just ate it up. There were so many days I just wanted to quit because I felt so bad."

But Michelle Akers has never been a quitter. To survive the effects of her illness she needed to adapt her lifestyle for the times when chronic fatigue would deplete her energy. No longer could she bulldoze her way through obstacles in her path. She also needed to adopt a new mental outlook.

Michelle read everything she could about her illness and sought the advice of doctors and nutritionists who specialized in CFS. She made radical changes in her diet by eliminating beef, caffeine, sugar, dairy products, and gluten flours. As a young, healthy athlete Michelle could run for hours, but now she needed to listen to her body's signals. If she awoke feeling ill, she stayed in bed and waited for another day to train. She also received a divorce from her husband and ended an unhappy four-year marriage that was draining energy she could not afford to lose. Over time she has noticed peaks and valleys to her condition.

In the midst of learning to live with a lifelong illness Michelle rediscovered her Christian faith. "My illness brought me back to God," she says. "Everything in life happens for a purpose. My particular challenge has been to take these painful times and experiences and turn them into something beneficial. I have learned to appreciate and rely on friends and family and to understand my role as a Christian. My Christianity gave me strength and peace of mind."

As she nears the end of her brilliant soccer career, Michelle is prepared for new challenges. "I realize that I can't control everything that happens," she says. "But I have learned that I can handle whatever comes my way. It is important to hang in there and to never give up. This is not about running sprints, it is about running a marathon."

Ruben Gonzalez

Street Survivor

It is a bright day in June but the shadows of tall buildings shade the rooftop corners of Ruben Gonzalez's childhood home in the heart of New York City's Spanish Harlem. Although he is a racquetball legend now, he casts his memory back to the wild days of his youth. Standing on the roof of his old six-story tenement building, he divides the streets below into the gang-infested turf of his teenage days.

"When I was a boy this neighborhood was carved up into territories," he recalls. "My gang, the Harlem Blues, patrolled 110th, 109th, and 108th streets from Madison to Lexington. The Vice Roys and Young Lords had us covered on both sides."

Carefully Ruben stares at the six-foot gap between buildings and the dark maze of littered alleys below. "I've watched friends from the barrio (neighborhood) get stabbed, clubbed, and die of drug overdoses. I had friends who died jumping from roof to roof, chased by rival gangs. Sometimes I can't believe I survived it all."

But Ruben Gonzalez has done more than just

survive. For nearly two decades he has been the grand old master of the professional men's racquetball tour. From 1985 to 1990 Ruben was one of the top four players in the world. In 1988, at age thirty-six, he upset five-time champion Mike Yellen to become the oldest pro to receive a number-one ranking in his sport. He kept this top ranking for three years. In a sport that favors youth and power, Ruben relies on intelligence, quickness, and a never-say-die spirit that he learned surviving his years on the street. For nearly twenty years he has been one of the most popular players on the tour, willingly signing autographs and offering tips for fans and fellow players. With money earned from endorsements, teaching at clinics, and tournament victories, he has provided a good life for his family and moved from the old neighborhood to a comfortable home on Staten Island.

It was the search for a better life that caused Ruben's father, Lumen Mendez, to move his family from Puerto Rico to New York City when Ruben was just an infant. The family lived in a small apartment in a six-story building on a busy street. Ruben's father worked hard to provide for the family, but his job as a custodian paid very little. They had a roof over their heads, food, and clean clothing, but not much more.

Ruben's whole world was the six-block area of his neighborhood. All day and into the night kids played such street games as stickball and stoopball. Everyone

Ruben knew spoke Spanish, and no one had much money. "It was a happy neighborhood in many ways," Ruben remembers, "but all my friends were poor; that was the only life we knew. When I needed new shoes, we could never afford them. I'd have to glue the old ones back together."

On the way home from elementary school each day, Ruben passed garbage-strewn empty lots and abandoned cars. Homeless people slept curled up in blankets under overpasses. Drunken men staggered down the street begging for money. "Almost every day I saw men shooting drugs into their arms in my stairway," Ruben says sadly. "I would jump over them and say, 'Excuse me' to get upstairs to my apartment."

As a young boy Ruben learned he had to be tough to survive. Gangs cruised the neighborhoods, and if you were not a member you risked being mugged or beaten. There was strength and protection in numbers, so Ruben joined his neighborhood gang, the Harlem Blues, at age 11. "I'm ashamed to tell you some of the things we did," he says. "To protect ourselves we used chains from playground swings. We carried knives and zip guns and were not afraid to use them. But underneath, I was scared stiff."

When he was fifteen his family decided to return to Puerto Rico, but Ruben refused to go. In his eyes the Harlem Blues offered a life of adventure and fun, and that is what he chose. By ninth grade he had quit school and was working all day packing and delivering groceries for a dime a bag. After work he joined the twenty members of his gang.

"When the sun went down we hung out in the park drinking beer, playing cards, and looking for action," Ruben explains. "If one of our members was beaten up we would track down whoever was responsible and then retaliate. I was in fights all the time. I survived by sheer luck."

When the clock struck 3 a.m. Ruben and his pals would call it a day. Sometimes he slept in a room at his grandmother's apartment. Sometimes he crashed on the floor of a friend's house or in the gang's clubhouse in the park.

Near the clubhouses of local gangs, in these little neighborhood parks, there were often one-wall handball courts. It was there that Ruben showed his real talent as a gifted athlete and fierce competitor. Because he was a school dropout, Ruben had no access to organized sports like football and baseball. Instead, he concentrated on one-wall handball, a game very popular in New York City at the time.

Ruben quickly became a handball phenomenon. Crowds of spectators six rows deep would "ooh" and "aah" as he leaped across the concrete court with little apparent regard for his body. He won dozens of trophies and spending money by placing bets on his games, but that was not what kept him going: It was all about self respect. For once Ruben Gonzalez felt good about himself. He was a somebody.

On weekends Ruben would take on all handball comers, riding the subways throughout the city to challenge neighborhood kingpins. His journeys around New York introduced him to a mix of different people and ways of life. "It opened my eyes to life outside the barrio," he says. "I began to realize that sports might help me make a better life for myself and my family."

One of the people Ruben met was tournament organizer and handball historian Mickey Blechman. "Ruben could have been a success in any sport, because his heart is three times the size of anyone else's," says Blechman. "He never cheated or complained. From the day he showed up he went after everything."

According to Blechman, a match Ruben played with Steve Sandler, the top one-wall player for years, demonstrates why Ruben is still considered a handball great. During a grueling match between the two, Sandler slammed a near-perfect shot off the right edge of the court. In a typical acrobatic display, Ruben jumped over four rows of spectators perched in lawn chairs and somehow returned the shot. Sandler, though he was stunned, sent another shot screaming off the wall. Ruben vaulted back over the spectators again, onto the court, and proceeded to nail a perfect kill shot to end the rally.

Although he was king of the courts, Ruben realized that the pocket money he picked up playing handball and the dead-end jobs he worked during the week would not pay the rent. Knowing that he had a wife and infant son to support, some of his handball buddies persuaded Ruben to take a job at an athletic club in Staten Island and learn a new sport: racquetball. With few other job options to help provide for his family, Ruben made the two-hour commute each way to work the desk at the club.

At the age of twenty-five, Ruben stepped onto an indoor racquetball court for the first time. Using a stubby five-dollar racket, he pounded the ball up to six hours each day to master the tricky angles and bounces of the four-wall game. Upon returning to his apartment building each night, he remembers, "I'd climb to the roof and swing my racket hundreds of times crying, 'God, please make me good at this!'" Within two years he was entering and winning regional tournaments and bringing home up to $200.

Encouraged by his success as an amateur, Ruben joined the professional racquetball tour in 1981. He soon realized that at 5-foot-9 and 160 pounds he could not match the power strokes of his younger, stronger opponents. Rather than try to out-muscle opponents who possessed 170-mile-per-hour serves, Ruben brought his street smarts and survival instincts to the game. "The way I see it," he says, "that court is my territory. When I step out there, I'm thinking, 'This guy's trying to take food from my table . . . no way!' I never give up, because I remember what it's like to be hungry. I carry that hunger and aggressiveness of my youth onto the court with me."

After a few years on the tour Ruben became known for his never-say-die determination. He went after every shot as if his life depended on it. In 1985 he also became known for the honesty and fair play that have earned him four Sportsman of the Year awards. In search of his first pro tournament win, Ruben was locked in a five-game battle for first place with long-time champ Marty Hogan. The match was tied at two games apiece. In the 11-point tie breaker, Hogan jumped out to an 8-0 lead, but Ruben charged back to tie it at 8-8. Both players were diving across the floor, grunting and groaning with each shot. Hogan grabbed the lead at 10-8, needing only one point to claim the tournament title. He served a bullet to Ruben's backhand, which began another furious volley. The rally ended when Ruben drilled home a forehand kill shot to regain the serve and a chance to win.

Fellow pro Jerry Hillecher explains what happened next: "Ruben overruled the ref and called a skip (the ball touched the floor before hitting the front wall) on himself. No one there could believe it. It was unheard of. It gave Ruben lasting respect from the other players and the fans. His message was that winning is not as important as honesty and having pride in yourself." Although Ruben eventually lost the match to Hogan, the battle launched his career as a rising star in the sport.

Returning to his old neighborhood on a beautiful spring day, Ruben Gonzalez is greeted by hugs, handshakes, and high fives. People who once crossed the street to avoid his menacing presence now call him Mr. Gonzalez and ask for his autograph.

"Sports was the way I used to become someone," he says between nods and waves to old neighbors. "Everyone has a special talent they can use to succeed just like I did, but not everyone does. So many of my old friends never made it. Some are still in prison and others are dead from drugs or the victims of violence. It could be me, I always think . . . it could be me."

Gail Devers

A Sprinter's Close Call

Her pillow is drenched in sweat from the fever and restless tossing. The searing pain in her feet burns a path up her legs. She squeezes her eyes shut, grits her teeth, and grips the quilt, holding on for dear life. Throwing the covers back, she lifts her head to study the source of this terrible pain. "Oh my God," she whispers in horror. "Oh my God."

Purplish blood blisters cover her feet and legs, oozing yellow fluid onto the sheets. Swollen to four times their normal size, her feet and legs are hideous—the stumps of some repulsive swamp monster, not the powerful muscle and bone of a world-class sprinter and hurdler. It is hard to remember after nearly three years of worry, fear, and suffering, but she is Gail Devers, a member of the 1988 U.S. Olympic team—one of the fastest women in the world. Just three years before, she ran 100 meters in less than 11 seconds. Prancing like a gazelle through the bramble and bush, she set a record for the 100-meter hurdles that same year. But today she lies in bed and cries, "It can't get any worse."

On these long, sleepless nights Gail lies awake and wonders why her life has come to this. After all, life was kind to her when she was growing up in San Diego. Her father, a Baptist minister, and mother, a teacher's aide, planned picnics, bike rides, and outings that kept the family close. Gail was a good student who longed to be an elementary school teacher so she could help other children. She had many interests, but sports was not high on her list until her brother beat her in a foot race.

"My brother used to make fun of me when he beat me in races," she says. "I decided I wasn't going to lose anymore, so I started practicing on my own. I beat him, and he never raced me again. From then on, running and track were all that mattered."

As a sophomore at Sweetwater High School, Gail was often the only girl representing her school in track and field meets. In one sectional event she won the San Diego girls' title for her school all by herself, winning a number of events. Despite the fact that her school had no coach, Gail was ranked as one of the fastest high school runners in the country. Based on her strong academic record and athletic talent she received a scholarship to UCLA, where she would work with a top-notch coach, Bobby Kersee.

Under Coach Kersee's watchful eye Gail learned the proper footwork needed to leap over the 33-inch hurdles. By her sophomore year she was gaining recognition as one of the top hurdlers in the country. She also learned how to burst out of the starting blocks in the 100-meter sprint, and by her junior year she was ranked second in the nation. In 1987 Gail won the 100-meter titles at the U.S. Olympic Festival and the Pan American Games.

In her senior year in 1988, Gail set a national record in the 100-meter hurdles with a time of 12.61 seconds. With the Olympics just a few months away, Gail was considered one of the nation's best hopes for Olympic gold in the hurdles and a challenger in the 100-meter dash.

But when she arrived in Seoul, South Korea, for the 1988 Summer Olympics, Gail began to feel ill. Although she could not define what was wrong, she knew she did not have the energy and drive needed to win. In the quarterfinals of the 100-meter hurdles she finished fourth, barely qualifying for the next round. In the semifinal race she finished last with a time of 13.51 seconds, her slowest since high school. Her poor performance eliminated Gail from further competition. Disappointed and confused, Gail began to doubt herself. "I remember thinking, 'Maybe I've overtrained this year and I'm tired. Maybe I was not prepared for the stress.'"

She returned home to the United States, where her symptoms grew progressively worse. Her skin was dotted with white patches that would peel off. Her hair would fall out in clumps whenever she brushed it. She suffered throbbing headaches and blurred vision, making it nearly impossible to study. She battled insomnia and constant exhaustion. Although she pursued her degree in sociology at UCLA, she could no longer train or continue her athletic career.

Throughout this puzzling ordeal Gail consulted teams of doctors who performed batteries of tests. Every inch of her body was poked, prodded, X-rayed, and examined. But the doctors were confused by her symptoms and could not figure out what was wrong. Some doctors even suggested that the problem was in Gail's mind and that she was not really sick at all.

For two and a half years the symptoms continued with no real answers. "It was depressing and frustrating not knowing what was wrong," Gail remembers. "Some of my friends thought I was on drugs because I lost so much weight and looked so bad. My skin was so disfigured that I covered all my mirrors so I wouldn't have to look at myself. When I went out in public people either stared at me or looked away quickly. Little children would come up to me, point and say, 'Mommy, what's wrong with her?'"

A once proud athlete who relied on her body, Gail came to feel as if her body had let her down. At 5-foot-3, Gail's best weight for running was around 115 pounds. During her long illness her weight would drop as low as 82 pounds and then might rise as high as 140 pounds. It was just another mysterious symptom in her undiagnosed condition. Out of sheer frustration Gail visited a friend of hers who was a doctor. The friend, alarmed by her appearance and symptoms, recommended another doctor. Fortunately this doctor understood Gail's condition. He explained to her that she suffered from Graves disease, a condition of the thyroid gland that affects nearly thirteen million Americans.

The thyroid is a small gland on the left side of the neck that performs several important jobs. It releases chemicals called hormones, which control body metabolism, the nervous system, and the muscles. In Gail's case the thyroid was enlarged to almost twice its normal size, and her illness had become so unusually severe that the treatment would have to begin with a procedure to shrink the enlarged gland.

To shrink her thyroid Gail had to endure a series of radiation treatments that made her even more violently ill. To neutralize the effects of the radiation, Gail was told to take a medication known as a beta-blocker. Because some athletes in the past had used certain drugs that contained beta-blocking substances to unfairly improve their ability to perform, all beta-blocking drugs were banned in the Olympics at that time. Any athlete found with a beta-blocker in his or her system, even someone with a serious medical condition such as Gail's, was banned from competition. Because she still hoped that she might recover in time to compete in the Olympics, Gail refused to take her beta-blocking medication. This decision proved costly.

The powerful effects of the radiation were eating away at the tissues in her body. Her immune system was in such a weakened state that it could not protect her. Gail did not understand what was happening to her body. "My feet were swollen to the point that I could not use my own shoes. I had to walk around in socks or men's slippers. When I pulled off my socks the skin came off with it," she explains. Although the memory is bitter, Gail recalls her darkest hour: "Having to crawl on the floor to the bathroom was the lowest I ever felt. The pain was excruciating. I thought for sure that I would lose my feet."

Lowering herself carefully to the floor, Gail crawls toward the bathroom, leading with her elbows, her feet sticking up in the air. She tries not to brush her feet against anything because the slightest touch sends shivers of pain through her body. "If I can just hold on," she thinks, but the pain floods through her and all is dark.

When she awakens in a hospital bed Gail sees the worried faces of her parents bent over her. In quiet voices Gail's parents and doctors explain the situation. The radiation treatments have lowered her resistance and a dangerous infection is now ravaging her body.

If she does not improve in two days the doctors fear they will have to amputate her legs to save her life. While her father leads the family in prayer, Gail fights for her life from her hospital bed. Not even Gail dares to dream of her athletic career. It will be a miracle if she ever walks again, let alone compete in another Olympic race.

The Devers family's prayers were soon answered as Gail miraculously turned the corner, fighting off the infection sufficiently to be able to return home. At first her feet were so badly damaged that she needed a wheelchair to move around the house. To help with the recovery process, her parents moved in with her. She had to be carried to the bathroom and bathed by her mother. Coach Kersee persuaded Gail to work out, and three weeks after returning from the hospital she surprised everyone by arriving in sweat socks to ride a stationary bike. Through painful first steps she learned to walk again and then to jog on the same UCLA track where she had been the university's athlete of the year in 1987 and 1988. Her new medication reduced the swelling in her feet, allowing her to wear her favorite track shoes.

In May 1991, after three years away from the track, Gail competed in her first race. She did not win, but she flashed enough of her old speed and form to excite Coach Kersee and herself. But as pleased as she was, Gail would never be satisfied until she worked her way back to the Olympics.

Now that she had returned from death's door, Gail trained with new enthusiasm. Her times continued to improve throughout the summer and fall. In a September 1991 race in Germany, Gail set an American record in the 100-meter hurdles at 12.48 seconds. Thanks to her new medication, a better diet, more rest, and her rigorous training, Gail's career was back in full swing.

At the U.S. trials for the 1992 Summer Olympic Games in Barcelona, Spain, Gail placed second in the 100-meter sprint and first in the 100-meter hurdles. She made the team and would race in both events. In the 100-meter dash Gail was not expected to win even a bronze medal. It was a strong field and she was happy just to be there. But Gail breezed through the qualifying races and lined up at the starting blocks with the gold medal at stake. The starter's gun sounded and the world's fastest women burned down the track in a blaze of furiously pumping arms and legs. Three sprinters flew across the finish line in a flash, so close together that a photograph was needed to determine the winner. The runners waited nervously for several minutes until the stadium announcer's words declared:

"The winner of the 100-meter dash, in 10.82 seconds: Gail Devers, USA."

Gail was elated with her unexpected victory, but she still had to prepare for the 100-meter hurdles. In the finals of the hurdles Gail blew out to a huge lead.

But her leg brushed against the final hurdle and she tumbled. She crawled to the finish line in fifth place. The loss was devastating, but after surviving a battle with Graves disease that nearly claimed her legs, if not her life, she was able to place it all in perspective. "Everyone has obstacles in life or days when it feels like the walls are closing in," she says. "During these times you must reach deep inside and find the inner strength to go on. You can never give up on yourself because you're the only one who can really help yourself. There is no doubt that it is hard, but it is worth the struggle."

Over the next four years Gail dominated women's track and field. Taking a daily dose of synthetic thyroid medicine helped keep her lifelong illness in check. She raced all over the world, landing world and national championships and toting home numerous women's athlete of the year awards. In the 1996 Olympic Games in Atlanta, Gail earned another gold medal as a member of the U.S. 4-by-100-meter relay team. Running in the 100-meter dash finals, Gail crossed the finish line in a pack of three, separated by an inch or perhaps the length of the long red fingernails that help identify her.

Pacing the infield of the track, waiting for the final results, she thinks back to the photo finish of 1992. "This is nothing new," she thinks. "I won in Barcelona, I beat Graves disease. Close calls are my specialty." She looks into the stands and spots her mother, clutching her hands in silent prayer. And then the announcer's voice rings out across the quiet stadium.

"Defending her title in the 100-meter dash, the winner once again: Gail Devers."

Gail Devers

Jim Eisenreich

This Is Who I Am

The kids stand in bunches outside the school, waiting to enter their fifth-grade classroom. Eleven-year-old Jim Eisenreich talks quietly with his friend Mike. A nearby group of girls points and snickers. "Oooh, there's Snorky. Make your piggy noises for us, Snorky," a girl shouts at Jim. The pack of girls laughs loudly. "Do you have the shakes again today, Snorky?" another girl asks. Jim lowers his head in shame.

"Ignore them, Jim. They don't know what they're talking about," Mike advises his best friend. But it's hard to ignore the teasing, name-calling, and mimicking that seem to follow him everywhere. Jim does not understand why his neck jerks suddenly to the side, or his face muscles twist and contort as if they have a life of their own. He holds his breath to stifle those snorting sounds that make it seem as if he is always clearing his throat. If he could stop the grunting that earned him the name Snorky he surely would—but he can't.

Jim remembers the time his father asked his mother, brother, and sister to leave the kitchen so he and Jim could have a heart-to-heart talk. "Why are you making those faces and noises, son? What's wrong with you?" his concerned father asked.

The tears stung Jim's face as he answered, "I don't know why I'm doing these things, but I can't help it."

Up until he was seven or eight years old Jim had experienced no symptoms. Then the eye-blinking started. His eyes would blink nonstop for long periods. Before long, other unusual symptoms appeared. His face muscles would twist suddenly, or his shoulders would shrug up and down. His hands trembled and shook slightly, and his neck and head would jerk to the side. His parents were worried, so they dragged him to many doctors, hoping to learn why he behaved so strangely.

Although the doctors examined him thoroughly, they were unable to place a name on his condition. One doctor claimed Jim was hyperactive and needed tranquilizers to calm him down. Another doctor declared that Jim had nervous tics that he would soon outgrow. "There is nothing seriously wrong with him," the doctors told the Eisenreichs.

In school Jim would get in trouble sometimes because teachers thought the noises and movements were his way of distracting the class. But having everyone watch him was the last thing Jim wanted.

Many kids made fun of him and others just stayed away as if they might catch whatever was wrong with him.

But whenever Jim felt really low, there were always sports to pull him out of a rut. Jim loved all sports, but he was especially drawn to hockey and baseball. When he played, the tics were still there, but no one seemed to pay attention. Instead, they noticed what a talented athlete Jim was. In baseball he could run like a deer and hit better than anyone in his hometown of St. Cloud, Minnesota. *Someday, maybe I can play for the Minnesota Twins,* he dreamed.

The twitching and grunting continued through middle school and high school, but those who knew him came to accept that it was just part of Jim. After graduating from high school he attended St. Cloud State College, where he developed into a graceful outfielder and explosive hitter. In 1980 Jim received word that his lifelong dream was about to come true: He had been selected by the Minnesota Twins in the annual draft of amateur players.

Jim was so excited to be a Twin that he left college early and quickly signed a contract. After just a year and a half in the minor leagues, Jim was invited to the Twins spring training camp in 1982. Despite the fact that he had played only in the lower minor leagues, the Twins decided to make him their opening day centerfielder. He rewarded the team with a blazing start to the season, but the tics and twitches that teammates noticed in spring training seemed to be showing up more often. Try as he might, Jim could not push the noises, shrugs, and convulsions down.

In the sixth inning of a home game against the Milwaukee Brewers on April 30, 1982, Jim seemed caught up in a strange outfield dance between pitches. He darted in quick, short steps to the left, then to the right. After pitches he would turn his back to the infield. He shook and twitched, holding his breath in the hope he could suppress the tics. Gasping for air, he called time and ran off the field. He was frightened, embarrassed, and confused about what was happening. "I was scared," Jim admits. "The tics had never been that bad before. I thought I might pass out and maybe even die."

The same thing happened in each of the next four games. Jim left the field in confusion and anger at himself for not being able to control the tics. By the time the Twins arrived in Boston for a road game, word had gotten out about Jim's struggles. The bleacher fans were merciless as they mocked him and screamed, "Shake, shake, shake!" This time he was forced to leave in shame in the second inning.

When the team returned to Minneapolis, Jim was put on the disabled list, and he checked into St. Mary's Hospital for tests. Once again there were differing opinions about Jim's condition, but the doctors narrowed it down to three possible causes. It was possible, some doctors claimed, that Jim had a form of stage fright; perhaps he was scared to perform in front of a large crowd. Another possibility was that Jim had agoraphobia, a fear of open places. Stage fright and agoraphobia are psychological disorders. In other words, something in the mind or way of thinking causes the problem. But the third possibility was a physiological or body disorder called Tourette syndrome. Scientists suspect that Tourette syndrome is caused by chemical imbalances in the brain that force the body to react with involuntary muscle contractions. Researchers believe that the brain releases a chemical at the wrong time, or that signals from one nerve to another are not processed correctly by those afflicted with Tourette syndrome.

Jim was greatly relieved to discover that there was finally an explanation for the condition he had suffered with for so long. The Twins management, however, did not accept the diagnosis of Tourette syndrome. Their doctors insisted Jim was battling psychological demons. "It's all in your mind," he was told. For the next three years, at the Twins insistence, Jim met with psychologists, psychiatrists, hypnotists, and experts in biofeedback. These specialists worked with Jim on training his mind to relax and to enjoy playing professional ball. But the problem was not in Jim's mind; it was in the signals his brain sent to the various parts of his body.

At the same time he was seeing the specialists recommended by the Twins, Jim read all he could about Tourette syndrome. He experimented with various doses of medicine to treat the symptoms, consulting with a doctor each step of the way.

According to the Tourette Syndrome Association, there are two hundred thousand Americans diagnosed with the condition, but there are likely several million undiagnosed sufferers. Like Jim, those with Tourette syndrome often must endure involuntary tics and muscle contractions that cause sudden, jerking movements. They may make grunting, snorting, or barking sounds over which they have no control. Some people with Tourette syndrome shout obscenities and call out words or phrases they cannot hold back. Although the condition is not life threatening, it can be humiliating for those afflicted.

Jim tried to play again during his rookie year but found that the tranquilizers he was given to calm the tics made him too drowsy to play well. After playing only thirty-four games, he quit for the year and returned home to try and make sense of his struggles.

By spring training of 1983 Jim was excited about giving it another try. But with little relief from the medications, Jim continued to feel the Tourette syndrome symptoms. Frustrated, he packed his bags and went home after just two games.

Back in St. Cloud, Jim starred on an amateur

baseball team and worked part time in an archery shop. He started the 1984 season with the Twins but decided to retire when he realized the symptoms were still haunting him on the field. It was devastating to let go of his lifelong dream, but Jim felt he had no choice.

For all of 1985 and 1986 Jim lived in St. Cloud, played amateur baseball, and continued to learn about Tourette syndrome. "For the longest time I thought I was alone with this problem," he says. "When I came to understand that I had Tourette's, I began to accept myself better. Once I accepted that Tourette's is part of who I am, I was able to build my self confidence. I realized that Tourette's is not the worst thing in the world, and then I was able to carry on with my life."

By the end of 1986 the Twins and most of the baseball world had given up on Jim Eisenreich, but an old friend in the Kansas City Royals organization was willing to give him one last chance. Armed with a much better understanding of his condition, Jim was ready to resume his career. He began 1987 in the Royals minor-league system, but his hot bat brought him back to the majors by mid-year. Although he still had some tics while playing, the combination of daily medicine (which he still takes to this day) and his own acceptance of the problem helped Jim deal with Tourette syndrome.

Since 1987 Jim has enjoyed a long, successful career as a valuable member of the Royals, Dodgers, Phillies, and Marlins. In 1996 he batted .360 for the year. He has smacked two home runs in World Series games and earned the respect of fans and fellow players. In 1996 he was named by *USA Today* as a Most Caring Athlete for his work helping children with Tourette syndrome. He is a national spokesperson for the Tourette Syndrome Association and meets frequently with groups of children to share his experiences.

Based on his experiences, Jim often tells listeners, "Just because you have Tourette's does not mean you are not as good as everyone else. Everyone in life has obstacles to overcome. Everyone in life is different. Learn to accept your differences and you can enjoy a normal, happy, and productive life. I know I did."

John Lucas
One on One

A man in a rumpled suit rubs his bloodshot eyes, rolls over on his side, and stares blankly at the deserted alley. "I had come to from a cocaine blackout," he explains years later. "I was coming off a binge in downtown Houston at 7 a.m. I was looking for my car, but I couldn't remember if I had driven it. I was trying not to be recognized, but there I was with shades on, filthy in my suit, urine all over my pants, no shoes, five pairs of socks on my feet, and I don't remember anything about the night before."

As he hauled up his exhausted body and tried to hail a cab, he prayed that no one would notice him. After all, he was no back-alley drug fiend; he was John Lucas, a professional basketball player for the Houston Rockets. He had been a number-one draft pick in 1976 and was still one of the top point guards in the game. He was a family man, too: the father of two young children, and husband to a loving and devoted wife. He was a respected member of his community with a beautiful house, expensive cars, and hand-tailored suits.

So why was this man who seemed to have it all staggering wearily down the street in the early morning hours of March 15, 1986?

The night before, like so many other nights in the past eight years, John's wife, Debbie, had locked the double-bolt doors from the inside so her husband could not escape to wander the streets in search of drugs. More and more often John had executed an escape, only to return at dawn claiming he was "out with the guys." He slept all day but always looked exhausted, with dark, brooding eyes. Money left lying around the house suddenly disappeared, and John spent long periods in the bathroom, locked away from his family. He roamed nervously from room to room, peeking out from behind windows with curtains tightly drawn. "Someone is out to get me," he thought. John Lucas was on the run from his teammates, his family, and most of all, from himself.

From early childhood on John was always doing one sort of running or another. He practiced basketball by shooting aluminum-foil balls into wastebaskets and guarding his sister as she maneuvered around the furniture. His parents, both principals of schools in the Durham, North Carolina, area, valued education but also realized the benefits of sports. They sent John to summer sports camps starting in third grade. "I never really spent a summer like most kids do," he recalls. "I never climbed trees or went fishing. To this day I still don't know how to swim. I didn't have any free time that wasn't involved with sports. I never had a lot of friends, just teammates."

While still in elementary school, John excelled in tennis tournaments around the state. Being the only African-American player at these tournaments throughout the South was uncomfortable, but John learned to stifle his nervousness and anxiety so he could concentrate on winning. "To me, winning wasn't everything, it was the only thing," he says. "That meant there was no such thing as compromise in my life. I either won or I lost—there was nothing in between. I never talked about my feelings, but inside I had lots of fears."

In seventh grade he started on the junior varsity basketball team and led the city in scoring. He starred every winter, including his senior year in high school when he averaged thirty-five points a game and led his team to the state tournament. As a tennis player, he battled stars like Jimmy Connors and Vitas Gerulaitis, and he earned a place on the U.S. Junior Davis Cup team. By the time he graduated high school John was a two-sport All-American with scholarship offers from hundreds of colleges.

After years of adult praise for his athletic accomplishments, John realized that sports provided more than the thrill of competition; it also offered a kind of athletes-only special treatment. At home, for example, John did not do routine chores such as washing dishes because his father did not want him to cut his hands. There was always someone to clean his room, wash his clothes, cook his meals, and smooth over any difficulties that might arise. When he attended the University of Maryland, the special treatment continued as he achieved collegiate All-American status once again in two sports.

As a star athlete John was catered to on all counts. Someone found him a place to live, provided for his daily meals, and made sure his sneakers were always in top condition or replaced if they started to wear. Years later, John came to realize how this treatment spoiled him. "You never learn to be responsible for yourself because someone will always do things for you," he says. "You never learn to grow as a person."

Throughout his childhood John proved he was something special in sports, but he grew up with the same insecurities and doubts as everyone else. Unlike most people, though, John did not learn the skills needed to deal with the ups and downs of daily life. "I was a teenager with pimples who was extremely self-conscious, but I never talked to anyone about this," John sadly remembers. "I realized at sixteen or seventeen that a drink could push painful feelings down. Before long I discovered that whenever I felt pain, sorrow, or hurt I could use drugs or alcohol to take those feelings away."

At the University of Maryland John won several conference tennis titles while leading the Terrapins basketball team each of his four years. The New Jersey Nets offered to draft him after his junior year, but John kept a promise to his mother and completed his education before joining the National Basketball Association. He was the first pick in the 1976 NBA draft. The day he signed his contract with the Houston Rockets he also signed a deal to play World Team Tennis with the Golden Gate Gators.

Being a professional athlete was not as glamorous as John had hoped. Professional basketball is a demanding job with games scheduled in different cities night after night. After games and practices John's teammates went their separate ways. Although he had been dating his future wife, Debbie Fozard, a girl who grew up only four blocks from his house in Durham and went through school with him, he lived alone, with empty hours to fill each day. At twenty-two John was convinced that he had already achieved most of his athletic goals. Out of boredom he began experimenting with cocaine and drinking more heavily.

On the court, however, John was clear-headed and sharp. About a third of the way through his rookie year he earned the starting point-guard job. With the Lakers' Magic Johnson checking him closely, John would dribble to the top of the key, fake a jump shot, and fire a bullet pass beyond Kareem Abdul-Jabbar's reach into the waiting hands of teammate Moses Malone. A thunderous dunk for two points by Malone gave John more satisfaction than hitting his own long jumper because he was a true floor general, setting up his teammates before considering himself. In his first season he made the NBA's All-Rookie team and was being counted on to lead the Rockets to a championship.

But during his second season in Houston the team suffered numerous injuries to key players and, despite John's strong play, they missed the playoffs. He was looking forward to helping the team rebound in his third season and was shocked to learn he had been traded to the Golden State Warriors in exchange for their star player, Rick Barry. John was hurt by the trade and concerned to be moving even farther from those he loved. By the start of John's fourth season, he was addicted to cocaine.

During the time John played for the Warriors his grandmother and his high-school coach both died, while both of his parents struggled with serious illnesses. John could not deal with the painful feelings of loss, so he buried his emotions in a downward spiral of drugs and alcohol. He was the Warriors' star player, ducking under Julius Erving for a layup or driving past Walt Frazier, but he repeatedly missed practices and airplane flights to games. Finally, the team suspended him without pay for the last twenty games of the season. Despite concerns expressed by John's wife, parents, and team, he denied that he had a drug problem, blaming his erratic behavior on a desire to play for another team.

John was traded to the Washington Bullets in 1981, but his drug problems persisted. By now Debbie Lucas realized that her husband's behavior was out of control, but she did not know how to help him. In John's autobiography, *One Day at a Time,* she says: "When John started having problems after he joined the Bullets, they tried to keep it hidden. When he missed practices or came late to a game they would say that John was having domestic problems. Well domestic problems weren't the problem; the problem was that he was out on a binge and didn't get home on time to get ready for practice. . . . I let John use me for a while, I know, but I didn't know what to do to help him."

There were more missed practices, flights, and games while he was in Washington, but John still denied the problem until a reporter released a story about his cocaine use. For several years he remained under the spell of cocaine. It destroyed his reputation and threatened to devastate his family. According to Debbie: "Both my daughter and son grew up around John's problem. One time John was passed out cold in the bathroom and my two-year-old son stood on his father's shoulders to use the toilet. Another time John came home and crawled into bed. Our son got into bed with him and put his arms around him as if to protect him. The kids cried for him when he didn't come home, or they'd grab onto him when he was going out, telling him to stay home. When he came back they would run to get him things—sodas and the like—to make him feel special."

When the newspaper story about John's drug problems appeared in 1982, he was forced to admit publicly that it was true. At the end of the season he attended an outpatient drug clinic in Virginia, but he continued to drink while being treated. He shrugged off the idea that his addiction was a disease. "I once thought an alcoholic or a drug addict was a guy who lived on a park bench," he admits. "I didn't know I could be an alcoholic and an addict. I thought if you could afford to buy the drugs, you didn't have a problem."

Next, John attended private sessions with a doctor and joined a six-week treatment program in Pennsylvania. But he refused to confront his feelings or analyze why he was attracted to drugs and drinking. He played along with the counselors and believed he could use sheer willpower to break his addiction at any time. Although he was sober for a number of weeks during the summer of 1982, within days of joining his teammates in basketball camp John was getting high again. He tried to hide his drug habit, but after missing practices and showing up late for games the team cut him nearly halfway into the season. Now very few teams would take a chance on John, so he was forced to play in the low-budget Continental Basketball Association. In 1983, the NBA's San Antonio Spurs, desperate for a point guard, signed him. Despite continuing his drug-and-alcohol lifestyle John was able to stay out of trouble through the season.

He signed with the Houston Rockets in 1984, but when the team tested him for drugs at the start of the season they found cocaine in his system. Once again he was suspended and enrolled in a drug-treatment program. This time, however, John admitted he had little control over drugs. All the same, he continued to sneak out of the house on his cocaine binges over the next two years. "I know now that it seems simple to just stop drinking or using drugs," John says, "but addicts cannot stop by themselves. Some people have to hit rock bottom before they can be helped. Many people die before they can receive the help they need." Waking up in a littered alley in downtown Houston in 1986 was John's rock bottom. "That night I think I was trying to get caught," he says. "I was too afraid to turn myself in, but I was sick and tired of living the way I was. I was desperate to get drugs out of my life. I wanted to be free."

When he entered a rehabilitation center for the fourth time, John brought a new determination with him. For the first time he was willing to confront painful feelings honestly and to admit to years of lying and deception. His counselors helped John face his emotions and rebuild damaged relationships with family members. Eventually, John came to understand how his selfish lifestyle had nearly destroyed his family and cost him everything. To overcome his addiction John had to eliminate the special treatment and me-first behavior that had ruled him since childhood.

"I needed to stop running away from life's problems and see that addiction is a problem bigger than me," John says. "Once I surrendered to God, a power much greater than myself, I was on the road to recovery."

While he completed his own treatment, John started a combination fitness and counseling program for substance abusers that many other athletes soon joined. He received thousands of letters and calls from drug abusers and eventually opened eight treatment centers. He resumed his basketball career and played until 1991, at which time he purchased a semi-professional team to help recovering players and coaches by providing counseling while they maintained their careers. Since then he has coached the San Antonio Spurs and Philadelphia 76ers, operated his successful drug treatment programs, and given speeches to thousands of young people.

John does not take his sobriety for granted. He attends daily Alcoholics Anonymous meetings and is committed to helping others find peace of mind without drugs and alcohol. “Don’t start drinking or using drugs,” he advises, “but if you have, you should know that your problems are not unique. Ask for help and know that you can get better. After all I have been through I am proud to say I am the best me I can possibly be.”

Mansour Bahrami

For the Love of the Game

He was born to play tennis. But he was born in a land where few but the rich and powerful were permitted to play. Mansour Bahrami was neither rich nor powerful. He was the son of a gardener who worked long hours for little money to feed his family of six. While his father labored at the sports complex in Tehran, young Mansour pressed against the chain-link fence and watched with wide eyes as wealthy Iranians lobbed balls back and forth over the net.

As a five-year-old he retrieved balls at the complex for a few cents an hour so he could be around this sport he loved. At the end of the day he returned to the family's one-room apartment in the slums of the city. The family was so poor that Mansour and his sister had to share an ice-cream cone on the two occasions a year his father could afford the treat. His father certainly could not afford to buy Mansour a tennis racket, so the boy played using a dustpan attached to a block of wood. He continued to work as a ball boy, and finally, at age twelve, he received his first real tennis racket.

But a lowly ball boy was not allowed to play at a fancy tennis club in Iran, so Mansour waited for his chance.

In the middle of a sweltering one-hundred-degree day the courts were empty, so Mansour and a friend sneaked on and proceeded to stroke the ball back and forth. Within a minute the fierce Iranian guards were upon them. "A guard lifted me above his head and slammed me to the ground," Mansour remembers. "I begged him to leave my racket alone but he smashed it on his foot. He beat me until I was bleeding from the face and head."

A less-determined boy would have given up the sport then and there, but Mansour continued to chase balls at the complex and hope that his fortunes might change. "I did not have much to eat or many clothes to wear," he says. "As long as I could be around the tennis club I was happy. I loved the game so much."

When the Iranian Tennis Federation became desperate to find new players to compete in international matches, they gave rackets to many of the ball boys and allowed them to use the courts. They did not, however, provide coaching, so Mansour learned by imitating others and creating his own unique shots. He could apply so much spin to the ball that it bounced first on his opponent's side of the net and then back to his side before it could be hit. As a teenager he played a few hours each day and developed a strong serve and accurate backhand and forehand returns to go with his assortment of trick shots.

Before long Mansour's persistence paid off as Iranian officials recognized his talent and added him to their Davis Cup team when he was only seventeen. Things were looking up for him now that he could play tennis daily, earn money by giving lessons, and face international competition with the Iranian team. The tennis federation even gave him a car to use and a house to live in.

At about this time the winds of political change were blowing throughout Iran. Under the leadership of the Shah, the government made many modern improvements in their attempts to compete in business with other nations, but conditions for the poor were shameful. According to Dr. John Voll, a Mideast scholar at Georgetown University in Washington, D.C.: "During the Shah's regime some people drove around in fancy cars while many others lived in shacks. Most of the money was used to build up the military or for government expenses while the poor were ignored and subject to miserable conditions. When the poor stood up for themselves they were punished severely."

Deeply religious Muslims who felt that the Shah's reforms were corrupt and sinful led protests and caused unrest in Iran during the 1970s. Led by the Ayatollah Khomeini, a religious revolutionary group overthrew the Shah's government in 1979 and proceeded to enforce strict new laws. "From 1979 to

1982 there was terrible chaos in the country," Dr. Voll explains. "It was unclear who was in charge of the country. Local revolutionary committees would roam the streets and arrest, torture, and kill people as they saw fit. Anything they thought represented the old days of the Shah was banned and done away with."

To the shock and disbelief of Mansour Bahrami and his fellow players, the sport of tennis was banned because the new government claimed it violated Islamic religious rules and traditions. For more than two years, during what should have been the prime of his tennis career, Mansour could not play or give lessons. He walked the streets aimlessly, watching in horror as his friends, neighbors, and family were arrested.

"Hundreds of thousands of people filled the streets," Mansour says. "If the government suspected that you did not agree with their policies you could be killed right on the spot. My eleven- and thirteen-year-old nephews were arrested along with thousands of others. I was anxious about the future. I could not imagine any work besides tennis."

Many Iranian citizens, including Mansour, attempted to leave the country at this time, but the borders were closed and almost no one was allowed in or out. Fortunately, Mansour knew someone who was friendly with the foreign minister. His friend spoke with the minister and, after months of waiting, Mansour was granted a passport and visas for travel to France and Switzerland. In August 1980 Mansour arrived in Nice, France, hoping to continue his tennis career. He was a newcomer in a strange land, though, and it took a long time to learn the language and adjust to a new way of life.

Eventually, Mansour made tennis-playing friends in France who helped him get part-time work giving lessons. Although he played and won many local tournaments, he earned just enough to survive, going two or three days at a time without food and walking the streets at night because he could not afford a room. With his travel visa due to expire in October 1980, Mansour lived in fear that he would have to return to the chaos of his homeland. Tennis friends in France helped him extend the visa a few more days or weeks at a time so he could remain in the country. The French government offered him a more permanent visa if he would formally declare himself a political refugee; however, that would mean he could never return to Iran and would never again see his family.

Torn by the passion to pursue his tennis career and the love of his family, Mansour decided not to accept political asylum in France. When his visa finally expired in February 1981, he was no longer legally permitted to stay in France. Nevertheless, he remained. "I was desperate," he says. "I could not return to Iran and be safe, so I walked the streets all night, hoping to avoid the police. I had no money, no home, and I felt I had no choice but to live like this until things changed."

His fortune changed when the French Open, a major professional tennis tournament, opened in Paris that May. Mansour entered the tournament as a wild card and shocked the tennis world by beating the third-ranked player in France while advancing far into the event. When the media discovered his story, it was publicized throughout the world. Many French politicians were sympathetic to his situation and felt the government should offer protection and safety for Mansour. Due to public pressure, he was soon given a new permit to live in France. The permit was updated several times.

Over the next five years Mansour played in France but was not allowed to play in professional tournaments around the world. At this time Mansour's homeland, Iran, was considered an outlaw nation by most other countries. Under the leadership of the Ayatollah Khomeini, Iran was accused of numerous acts of terrorism that resulted in death and destruction around the globe. Although he no longer lived in Iran, Mansour's Iranian citizenship caused many countries to refuse to let him play tennis within their borders. "It was incredibly frustrating to be shut out of these tournaments," Mansour notes. "I would apply for a visa to enter a tournament, but the country I applied to would tie it up in red tape until the tournament was over and then I could not play. I am sure I was discriminated against because of where I was born."

At age thirty, with his best tennis years behind him, Mansour Bahrami was finally permitted to join the men's professional tour as a full-fledged member. His highest ranking in singles play was only 192, but he was a top doubles player during the latter part of the 1980s, reaching the French Open doubles finals in 1989. In 1994 he was asked by Jimmy Connors to join the Nuveen Tour for players over thirty-five years old. Since then he has become one of the most successful and popular players on the tour because of his unusual and entertaining style. In a match against Bjorn Borg or John McEnroe, Mansour may wait for his opponent to serve by twirling his racket around his finger like an old Texas gunslinger. He has been known to hit a ball straight up in the air and then catch it in his pocket. While serving against Johan Kriek not long ago he crammed eight balls in one hand while serving with the other. In the midst of a furious volley he will suddenly return a shot between his legs or nail a behind-the-back cross-court winner that has his opponent stumbling over his own feet.

Unable to play the top competition of his era as a political exile in France, Mansour found new life playing against tennis legends on the Senior Tour. Facing such senior superstars as Connors and McEnroe, Mansour has been ranked in the top ten several times.

Mansour Bahrami

According to fellow senior player Tim Wilkerson, "No one knows for sure whether Mansour, in his prime, would have been another Jimmy Connors. Having played against him, I can say he certainly would have been one of the top players in the world had he been given the chance to compete when he was in his twenties."

Despite the fact that he was denied the opportunity to compete against the world's top players during his best years, Mansour is neither bitter nor disappointed. "I try not to look back at what might have been," he says. "The worst thing in life is to not be allowed to do what you love. If you fight for the things you love and believe you can achieve them, there is a good chance you will achieve your goals. I am a grown man making my living doing what I love: playing tennis."

Greg LeMond
Making a New Plan

The early morning woods were quiet this April day in 1987—the kind of quiet that lets a man think about his life. And that is what bicyclist Greg LeMond was doing. He was crouched in the brush, scanning the area for wild turkey and thinking about the past year. Somewhere behind him in these California woods, Greg's uncle and brother-in-law fanned out, shotguns in hand, ready to shoot at the first sign of movement. *It has all gone according to plan . . . so far,* Greg thought. *Winning my first Tour de France was a dream come true. In a few days I return to the grind of the tour, but for now life couldn't be sweeter.*

And then it happened! In a split second all the plans and dreams were laid to waste. "I stood up to see where the others were," Greg remembers. "I heard a gunshot go off. I saw blood coming out of my finger. I could feel blood fill up my lungs. I screamed! I got shot!"

When Greg moved in the bush below, Greg's brother-in-law had mistaken his camouflaged body for a turkey. He fired at Greg, spraying fifty-five pellets through his back and neck. As the life streamed out of him, Greg's hunting buddies desperately called for help and dragged him from the woods.

I'm dying. I will never see Kathy or my two-year-old again, Greg thought as he slipped in and out of consciousness.

An emergency helicopter, in the vicinity purely by chance, picked up the police call and touched down in a nearby field. By the time he arrived at the hospital, nearly three quarters of Greg's blood had drained from his body. Pellets had punctured his lungs, kidney, small intestine, liver, and the lining of his heart. Barely clinging to life, Greg was wheeled into the operating room for ten hours of surgery.

When Kathy LeMond saw her husband in the recovery room after his operation she could not believe her eyes. "He was hanging a few inches off the bed, suspended because they didn't want him laying on his wounds," she says. "He had so many holes in him he looked like a colander. I was just praying he would live."

Over the next four weeks there were times Greg must have wondered whether living was worth the constant pain. One minute he was shivering with cold, the next minute his body was overheating, soaking him in a layer of sweat. A nine-inch incision in his stomach made it impossible to move or talk. In a one-month period Greg lost twenty-five pounds, most of it the fine-toned muscle of a world-class athlete. It had taken years of planning and hard work to become the first American ever to win the Tour de France, and it was hard to watch it slip away.

Growing up in the Nevada countryside, miles from the nearest neighbors, Greg knew very little about bicycles or the great races of Europe. He loved solitary outdoor activities like skiing, hunting, and fishing, but had no interest in competitive cycling until a strange coincidence occurred one day in 1975. As he and his dad were leaving the house, they found themselves blocked in by hundreds of riders competing in the Northern California/Nevada State Championships. The longer they watched, the more fascinated they became with the idea of bicycle racing. Within a year, fourteen-year-old Greg and his dad had bought racing bikes and begun competing in and around the state.

Greg achieved success at every level he raced, often beating older, more experienced riders. In his first three years of amateur racing, Greg won more than half the races he entered. In 1979 he earned the highest honor possible for an amateur cyclist, winning the World Junior and National Junior Road championships. He also began to read cycling magazines, which filled his imagination with the history and tradition of the most popular sport in Europe. That same year, Greg signed his first professional contract and made the U.S. Olympic

Cycling team. The United States refused to participate in the 1980 Olympics in Moscow to protest the Russian invasion of Afghanistan, but Greg performed brilliantly as a rookie rider on the professional tour.

Each year Greg grew stronger and learned key strategies for road racing with aggressive European riders. When he finished the 1985 Tour de France in second place, it was obvious he was ready to make his mark. Sure enough, in 1986 Greg wore the winner's jersey in the most prestigious and exhausting cycling race in the world, the Tour de France.

Just months before the turkey shooting accident Greg could power past fellow racers as he climbed the switchbacks and steep inclines of France's Pyrenees mountains. Two weeks after the accident he needed to lean heavily on Kathy just to walk fifty feet before collapsing in exhaustion. Recognized as one of the best-conditioned athletes in the world, five weeks after the accident the best Greg could manage was a leisurely two-mile ride around the neighborhood. "I was worried about our future," Kathy admits. "What would we do if he couldn't ride again?"

The sport of cycling is big business in Europe, much like professional football, basketball, and baseball are in the United States. European sponsors had watched Greg closely as he rose through the amateur ranks, and then bid fiercely for his services when it became obvious that he was a genuine talent. The day he was shot, April 20, 1987, his sponsor heard the news and immediately stopped paying his salary, figuring Greg was no longer of any use to the team. Although he needed at least a year to heal from the serious injuries, Greg felt he needed to return to Europe right away to land a contract with a new sponsor. He rushed his recovery, and by July his training rides were up to three hours long. Just when things were looking up, Greg was floored once more by terrible pain in his abdomen. He was rushed to the hospital and underwent emergency surgery to clear a blockage in his intestine caused by scar tissue from his previous operation. Once again Greg was bed-ridden with a long scar on his stomach while his cycling career slipped away.

Before sponsors would offer Greg a new contract, they wanted to see him race to prove that his recovery was complete. In August, Greg flew to Europe and gave it his best shot. But his body could not handle the strain, and Greg would frequently drop out just a few miles into a race, drawing the intense criticism of coaches and reporters. "It took more than ten years to reach the level I had achieved, and to have that wiped out so quickly was discouraging," he says. "But I have always been a positive person, and I knew if I could stay focused and ignore the criticism I would make it back. There were times I was down, but when I woke up the next morning I was positive again."

Professional cycling is one of the most demanding sports in the world, and though Greg worked hard to regain top form, he struggled through the 1987 and 1988 seasons. Most cycling experts figured Greg's career was a thing of the past when he lined up for the 1989 Tour de France. Lasting over three weeks and winding around nearly 2,500 miles of the country, the Tour de France is raced in stages. Some stages are long mountain climbs that stretch out over a period of hours. Other stages are time trials or sprints in which riders pedal furiously, hoping to strip valuable seconds off the clock on a much shorter course.

During the 1989 Tour de France Greg surprised his many critics. By the final stage of the race Greg trailed race leader Laurent Fignon by fifty seconds. In a short stage, such as the Versailles to Paris 24-kilometer route that would end the '89 tour, it would be almost impossible to make up that time. The odds were stacked against Greg, but his career as a racer and his recovery from gunshot wounds had taught him some valuable lessons. "I learned to focus on what you can do, not on what people think you cannot do," Greg says. "No matter what you are facing, don't feel sorry for yourself. Set goals for yourself, aim for those goals, and then go all out to achieve those goals."

From the first pedal stroke, Greg went flat out. With his legs pumping furiously he soared through the streets of Paris in a record time of 26 minutes, 57 seconds. Along the way fans shouted his name, but Greg kept his focus on the road. He traveled the distance at thirty-four miles per hour, an unheard of speed in such a time trial. Laurent Fignon, as is the custom in a time trial, waited his turn and set out two minutes after LeMond, but he could not match Greg's incredible pace. At the finish line Greg waited anxiously with his eyes on the overhead clock, keeping track of Fignon's time. Fignon pedaled furiously, but in the end he could not keep pace and Greg won the overall race by a mere eight seconds, the smallest margin of victory in Tour de France history.

In the 1990 Tour de France Greg rode with his strongest team yet and once again finished first, etching his name forever in the record books as one of the all-time great riders. But after that victory Greg found the going much tougher. He tired easily and had to drop out of many races. Although he performed poorly for several years, it was not until 1993 that Greg learned the cause of his fatigue. Extensive medical tests showed that he suffered from a genetic muscle disorder called mitochondria myopathy. The muscles in Greg's body shut down during heavy periods of exercise because they did not receive enough fuel. The condition often left Greg feeling weak, as if he were fighting the flu or a virus. It spelled the end of Greg's competitive cycling career in 1994.

Although he feels fine most days, it is not clear what Greg's future will bring. According to his wife, Kathy, no one knows how physically able he will be by the time he is fifty, so Greg tries to do the important things he has always wanted to do while he still can. He has given much of his free time and energy to raise money for disabled people, riding in events at which he shares his positive message.

"Having gone through some traumatic things myself, I gained more empathy for people who have gone through hardships and trying times," Greg says. "I learned to appreciate how much I do have. As a rider I always tried to find what was right for me. I made a plan and followed it. But sometimes circumstances change everything and you have to learn to make a new plan. The same is true for all of us."

Greg LeMond

Diana Golden Brosnihan

Gliding on the Edge

Diana Golden Brosnihan's kitchen is a warm, bright, and cheerful place. On sunny days she sits at the table to watch the sun dance across the sparkling water of Bristol Harbor, Rhode Island. Sometimes the light passes through the stained-glass wall panel on her window, spreading an array of colors throughout the room. The colors splashed upon her walls are like the days of her life—sometimes radiant and aglow, sometimes dark and shadowy.

It was little more than a decade ago that Diana dominated the world of disabled skiing. In 1988 she was named the Female Skier of the Year by the United States Olympic Committee. In 1997 she was inducted into the International Women's Sports Hall of Fame. She is a legend on the slopes, but like any great skier she has crashed and fallen many times. Now, at age thirty-five, she is facing metastatic breast cancer that has spread to her spine, ribs, and pelvis.

It is the day after Thanksgiving, and Diana sits at her kitchen table reflecting upon what she is thankful for. "I am extremely thankful for my husband, Steve, who is generous, funny, and such a solid person," she says. "I am thankful for my Alaskan malamute, and for this wonderful house I live in." She pauses to gather her thoughts and then adds, "I am thankful there could be so much joy at a time that could be so depressing."

Much of Diana's early childhood in Cambridge, Massachusetts, was all about joy and happiness. She was the middle child in a close and active family that liked to spend winter vacations on the ski slopes of New Hampshire. "I was always full of energy and mischief," she says. "I was the one in the family who managed to knock my head on the radiator and needed to be rushed to the hospital for stitches in the middle of a blizzard."

Although she was full of spirit, Diana hated the competitiveness of organized sports and gym classes. She thrived on the individual nature of skiing and was shooting down ski trails by the time she was five. She treasured the sense of freedom and speed she found on her ski runs, and in high school was nicknamed "Kamikaze" for her reckless behavior on the slopes.

One day, when she was twelve, Diana was outside building a snow fort with her friends. When she ran back from the woods, her right leg suddenly buckled and sent her tumbling to the ground. The trouble with her leg persisted, so her parents took her to a series of doctors, hoping to identify the problem. Finally, a biopsy of her leg revealed that she had bone cancer. Surgeons would have to amputate her right leg just above the knee. "It was shocking," she recalls. "But then I asked if I could still ski and they said I could, so I knew I could do the things that mattered to me."

About a week after her operation, the doctors removed the artificial leg that had been placed where the real leg had been. "There was nothing there," she says. "To see that the first time was very upsetting. At dark times like that I have always had lots of support from friends and family. I cry a lot and then move forward."

Before long Diana was up, moving around, and finding that things were not so bad after all. Kids in her seventh-grade class who had been mean to her started treating her kindly. And best of all for Diana, she was no longer required to attend gym class. "I figured I had now been given the world's best excuse to get out of gym," she remembers with a giggle.

She learned to ski on one leg by working both edges of the ski in a rolling motion, which allowed her to turn and maintain balance. At first she used outriggers (forearm crutches with little ski tips on the end) to help her, but she soon ditched these for traditional ski poles, which are lighter.

Diana did not ski competitively until her junior year in high school. That is when David Livermore, the ski team coach, approached her. He convinced her to train for the sport by strengthening her abdominal, leg, and arm muscles. In training she pushed herself beyond what she thought were the limits of her endurance. Within a year her strength, stamina, and technique on skis were remarkably improved. By her senior year in high school Diana was competing in the World Games for Disabled Athletes in Norway.

Over the next decade Diana won ten World Championships and nineteen U.S. National Championships medals. In the 1988 Winter Olympics in Calgary, Alberta, she won the gold medal in the giant slalom event for disabled skiers.

"The thrill was skiing on the edge. The sensation of feeling the ski working underneath me was spectacular," Diana says. "There were times when I was in the zone that I felt like a flying machine, like a missile or an arrow flying down the race course."

Having only one leg on which to handle the slippery turns of events like the slalom presents many problems to a disabled skier. With only one ski there is little room for error, and it is harder to maintain balance. Furthermore, one leg fatigues faster than two and, in a longer race, the bounces and turns of the course place tremendous pressure on that leg. But Diana never viewed one-legged skiing as a problem. She loved the life of a ski racer—the complete focus on something that was her passion. She loved the ritual of preparing for the slalom, in which she knew she would likely nick the gates with her shoulders, arms, and face. Like a knight preparing for a joust, Diana would slowly dress in hockey chest pads, arm and leg guards, and a face guard. After the race she would proudly examine the bloody lip or bruises that had marked her effort as she sped down the hill.

When Diana's skiing career began, disabled athletes were considered by many as no more than a curiosity. "When I started it was thought of as, *Oh, isn't that cute, they're skiing—that's wonderful and so courageous,*" Diana explains. "But I didn't ski on one leg to be courageous. The commitment required to be an athlete is the same whether all your body parts are working or not." Outgoing and full of energy and enthusiasm, Diana became a spokesperson and role model for disabled athletes. She was a key figure in changing the way disabled athletes were viewed by the media, sponsors, and the public. Thanks to her efforts, future disabled athletes, like wheelchair marathon racer Jean Driscoll, were taken seriously and recognized for their hard work and pure athletic ability, not for the fact that they were disabled.

Even the training, which many athletes found torturous, was a joy to Diana. In the spring she would jog on crutches, swim long distances, lift weights, and hop the stadium steps at Dartmouth, where she went to college. During the ski season the work intensified, but Diana simply reveled in it. "Pushing beyond the limits of what I thought I could do made me think that with the simple power of will, vision, and commitment I could overcome anything."

After retiring from the ski world in 1990, Diana began making a living by giving motivational speeches. At that time, however, she learned that willpower alone could not overcome everything, as she learned that she had breast cancer. Although she had to endure more painful surgery and an exhausting routine of chemotherapy, Diana continued traveling the country to give inspirational speeches. The years of training and racing gave her the stamina to push forward, away from the darkness and fear, toward the light.

But four months after recovery, another medical concern forced doctors to remove her uterus and eliminate any chance that she would give birth to children. Try as she might, Diana could not shake the gloomy thoughts and low spirits that now followed her everywhere. She plunged into a deep depression and even considered taking her own life.

"Sometimes you have to delve into the darkness and not run away from it. You have to pass through the fear to find out what is beyond it," she says. "I learned from skiing to never give up. When I saw no light I still kept going. I knew I could find some way to survive."

Perhaps because she had fallen so many times on the ski slopes, Diana knew how to brush herself off and pick herself up. She spent long hours crying, talking with close friends, and coming to terms with her situation.

Then, in 1993, while still struggling to find the light, she added a frisky twelve-week-old malamute pup to her life. She named the dog Midnight Sun and, true to his name, the dog's bright and playful personality helped illuminate the darkest nights of Diana's despair.

After learning in 1996 that the cancer had spread to her skeletal system, Diana moved from Colorado back east to be near family and friends. She met Steve Brosnihan, her future husband, at a Halloween party, and soon fell in love and married him.

Despite the setbacks she has faced, Diana has climbed Mount Rainier, hiked alone in the high Utah desert, and climbed a frozen waterfall. She has raced down the mountain at 65 miles per hour on dazzling sunny days and fallen to the bottom in an agony of dark pain and despair. Diana's life has not been easy, but she has always lived it on her own terms.

Like Diana, each of us must face the challenges life presents, and make sense of it all in our own way.

Although she loves a romp in the woods with her dog and ballroom dancing with Steve, Diana has also discovered how to sit quietly while the sun splashes colors through the stained-glass panel in her kitchen. "Now," she says with a content sigh, "I have finally learned to slow down enough to watch the sunlight on the water."

Diana Golden Brosnihan

Chris Zorich
Zora's Gift

It is 3:00 p.m. and school is out for the day. Chris Zorich and his best buddy head to the candy store for a round or two of video games. Along the way they pass boarded-up storefronts and burned-out buildings. They cross the street to avoid the taunts of a tough-looking gang of boys. Carefully they step over prone bodies bundled in ragtag sleeping bags and overcoats. The South Side of Chicago is a rough place to grow up in the late 1970s, but at least Chris can escape to the fantasy world of video games.

In a minute he is safe inside the store, absorbed in his game. Suddenly he hears a crash. Chris sees two men with guns drawn. The store owner's face is pressed hard against the glass display case. The robbers bark orders at the cashier as Chris and his friend try to shrink away. But they are spotted by one of the gunmen. He aims his gun at them and shouts, "You kids—scram!"

Chris is lucky to escape another close call, but it will take more than luck to survive a childhood of violence, hunger, and poverty. It takes determination, hard work, and discipline to rise from these streets. And more than all that, it takes love to survive. For Christopher Zorich, it is the undying love and devotion of his mother that will carry him from the corner of 81st and Burnham to a life of All-America honors and a career in the National Football League.

Zora Zorich, Chris's mother, was of Yugoslavian descent. His father, who was African-American, left when he learned Zora was pregnant with Chris. As a biracial boy with a white mother living in a black neighborhood, Chris was a walking target for gang members. "I used to get beat up a lot just because my mom was white," Chris explains. "In my own neighborhood I was called white honkey. When I ventured into a white neighborhood I was called nigger."

No welcome wagon greeted the Zorich family to the neighborhood. Instead, they received hate mail and had bricks thrown through their windows. But Chris and his mother were too poor to live elsewhere so they stayed on the South Side despite the fact that their apartment was ransacked over and over.

"One time I came home from the store and the door was off its hinges," Chris says. "We laughed, though, because our house was full of roaches and mice but hardly anything else. There was nothing worth stealing. The burglar must have thought someone else had already robbed us."

And if his life was not difficult enough, Chris was also picked on for stuttering and for being so poor that he had to scrounge for meals by picking through garbage cans. Mrs. Zorich suffered with diabetes and could not stay on her feet long, so working a regular job was out of the question. She baby-sat and picked up odd jobs when she could, but they were forced to pay the rent and food bills with the meager amount provided by public assistance. Their refrigerator was usually bare, storing only bottles of ketchup and mustard. Many nights Chris was so famished that he went to bed early so he would not have to face an evening of hunger pangs. In the morning he would rush off to school to receive the free breakfast that would hold him for a while.

On nights that they did not eat at a shelter, the Zoriches waited until a supermarket closed so they could visit the alley in back of the store. "I would dig into the dumpster and pull out prewrapped packages of fruit, vegetables, and meat," Chris says. "Mom would cut off the rotten parts and we would salvage the rest. I know how much this hurt her, to lower her son in the dumpster, but my mom never let on that it was a problem."

Mrs. Zorich regretted having to scrounge for food and to frequent the Salvation Army to find clothes for Chris, but she would do anything to make life better for her son. She tossed footballs and baseballs to Chris in the park, and watched sports on television with him. Some of the kids laughed at Chris for playing ball with his mom, but the Zoriches ignored the teasing. She read to him, helped him with his homework, and taught him never to give up.

When Chris was ten he stuttered so badly that it was nearly impossible to read an essay to his class. As he stumbled through it, Chris could hear the giggles of classmates, and he sat down in humiliation, unable to finish. Mrs. Zorich helped Chris practice over and over at home until he could read the essay without a hitch. At the end of the school year Chris asked his teacher for a second chance, and—thanks to his mother's encouragement—he delivered the essay flawlessly.

Despite the hardships of her life, Zora Zorich kept a positive attitude and a generous, forgiving spirit because she knew Chris was always watching. Wherever they ate dinner she smiled and gave Chris her portions while she nibbled skimpy salads. Teenagers would offer to carry her bags from the store, but she refused and tipped them anyway, knowing how badly they needed the money. She rarely had a spare penny, but when she did Mrs. Zorich bought candy for the neighborhood children. When Chris left the house for school or to play with friends she was sure to shout, "I love you," and Chris was not embarrassed to call back, "I love you, too, Mom." They were a team of two and together they would survive the mean streets.

One winter day, as Chris and his mother were walking home, a group of kids attacked them with a barrage of snowballs. A snowball smashed Mrs. Zorich in the face, sending a tear trickling down her cheek. "When I saw her crying," Chris says firmly, "I made it my mission to get my mother out of this desolate place."

When he was a freshman at Chicago Vocational High School, Chris was approached by the football coach, who wanted the big boy to try out for the team. Although his mother objected at first, fearing Chris would be injured, by his sophomore year she allowed him to play. He relished the hard work and sense of belonging that the team provided. The bullies who once called him "Fat Boy" now stepped aside to let his muscled body pass. Perhaps he also welcomed the chance to push around someone else after years of being beaten by neighborhood tough guys.

By his junior year Chris was attracting attention from college scouts for his rugged play. "When I was being recruited by Notre Dame I agreed to attend before Coach Lou Holtz could visit my house," Chris says with a chuckle, "because I was afraid something might crawl across the floor while he was there."

During his first year in college Chris found the schoolwork difficult. He wanted to quit and return home, but he talked with his mother by telephone each night, and she convinced him he could succeed if he rolled up his sleeves and worked harder. "There is nothing for you to come back to here," she told him.

Chris applied himself fully in the classroom, and on the football field he was unstoppable. In his four years at Notre Dame, Chris became a dominant defensive lineman. Although considered undersized, he was known for his quickness, strength, and ferocious attitude. On the field Chris screamed at offensive linemen and snarled at tight ends trying to fend off his advances.

After a game against the University of Southern California, rival quarterback and future NFL player Todd Marinovich told *Sports Illustrated,* "Every time I walked up behind the center, Zorich was the guy my eyes went to. He's scary." Throughout his college career Chris played his best against the top-ranked teams, charging like a raging bull through opposing linemen. He played as if his life depended on it.

"If I did not get good grades in college or make it to the pros I knew I would end up back in the old neighborhood," he says. "If I could survive having a gun to my head, I could definitely handle the stress of a football game." He was named to the All-America team three years in a row and won the Lombardi Trophy his senior year as the nation's top college lineman. When Chris returned home for vacations and to visit his mother, the same kids who once threw snowballs at them were now throwing compliments his way.

Chris Zorich

On New Year's Day of 1991 Notre Dame lost to the University of Colorado in the Orange Bowl, but Chris was named the team's most valuable player. He played with the power of a roaring freight train, throwing down running backs and quarterbacks on the way to a ten-tackle, one-sack game. He thought of how proud his mother would be when he graduated from college in May. He was on the verge of accomplishing his mission: in a few months he would be drafted by the NFL and could move his mother from their dangerous neighborhood. After the Orange Bowl game Chris called to let her know when his plane would arrive in Chicago so she could meet him at the airport.

When the plane landed, however, Mrs. Zorich was not there. Chris hurried home and pounded on the apartment door, but there was no answer. He raced around to the back, pulled the screen off the bathroom window, and climbed inside. He found his mother lying on the hallway floor. Just hours before he arrived in Chicago his mother had suffered a heart attack and died. Chris bent down, kissed his mother, and whispered, "Bye, Mom. I love you."

A few months after the death of his mother Chris was drafted by his hometown team, the Chicago Bears. In the big, burly world of the NFL, a 6-foot-l, 275-pound lineman like Chris was considered small, but he refused to listen to the critics. "I brought a hunger to succeed to the game," Chris explains. "My mother taught me that you can accomplish anything if you set your mind to it. If you believe in yourself you can handle a huge offensive lineman and just about anything else."

Over his seven-year career with the Bears and the Washington Redskins, Chris made his mark as one of the toughest players on the football field. But it is his work off the field that would make his mother proudest.

Since his first year in professional football, Chris has returned to his old neighborhood regularly to lend a hand. He established the Care To Share program to give baskets of food to hungry families on the South Side. On Mother's Day Chris orders and delivers dozens of flower bouquets to neighborhood moms. And Chris accompanies boys and girls to cultural events around the city. To honor the memory of his mother, Chris created the Zora Zorich Scholarship Fund to help deserving disadvantaged students attend Notre Dame. Chris himself returned to the college after injuries forced him to retire from the NFL in 1997. While completing his law degree, Chris is actively involved in all Zorich programs, carrying groceries, ice-skating with eight-year-olds, and speaking in schools around the city.

"Although we had so little, my mother gave me so many gifts," Chris says. "I feel her spirit with me every day, showing me the way. These programs are my way of showing others the way."

Zina Garrison

No One Is Perfect

"There is no doubt about it," the sportscaster shouted above the crowd into his microphone. "Zina Garrison has shown the world, here at the 1989 U.S. Open, that she is at the peak of her game. She has just defeated the legendary Chris Evert and now is coming over to chat with us."

Zina Garrison looked calm and peaceful as she faced the television cameras, but a storm was raging inside her. Although she politely answered all the questions the sportscasters asked, she could barely squash the ugly thoughts that boiled inside of her. "This should have been an enormously happy time for me, but all I could think about was how awful I looked," she says, looking back on that day. "My face was splotchy, and I thought of myself as a person with a small upper body and the lower body of an elephant."

For nearly six years Zina kept a secret from the world. On the tennis court she was strong and confident, the greatest African-American woman player since two-time Wimbledon champion Althea Gibson. After upsetting Chris Evert, her ranking would rise to fourth in the world. Off the court, however, she suffered in silence with an eating disorder known as bulimia nervosa. In the confines of her hotel room, when no one was around, she consumed gigantic amounts of food and then forced herself to throw up so she would not gain weight. Her skin was marred with a constant rash. Her hair and fingernails were brittle, and the acid from her stomach (which her frequent vomiting brought up) was eating away at the enamel on her teeth. She was moody and depressed. Despite her great success on the courts, she often felt worthless as she jetted around the world from one tournament to another. She spent years striving to develop the perfect backhand, but that same drive for perfection, when it was turned on herself, only made her miserable. For no matter how hard she tried to be the perfect sister, daughter, or person, she could never meet her own expectations. In her mind she always fell short, and that was hard to live with.

Zina was born and raised in Houston, Texas. Her early life was happy, despite the fact that her father had died before she was a year old. That just drew her closer to her mother, four sisters, and two brothers.

Zina was a tomboy, tagging after her older brother Rodney to play baseball or ride bikes. One day, when she was ten, she followed Rodney to MacGregor Park to meet his tennis-playing girlfriend. There she met John Wilkerson, who encouraged her to play and soon became her coach.

"I have always liked things out of the norm," Zina says. "In my community it was unusual for an African-American girl to play tennis, and that was part of its appeal. In no time flat I felt I just had to play. I would cry if my mom said I could not play."

By the time Zina was twelve she was competing in state and national tournaments. In 1981, when she was eighteen, she was ranked as the top junior tennis player in the world. The day she graduated from high school she stepped onto an airplane and flew to Paris to make her professional debut in the French Open. Within two months of turning pro, Zina was ranked tenth on the women's tour. There was no doubt about it, she was sitting on top of the world. But then her whole world fell apart.

In 1983 Zina's mother died suddenly from complications of diabetes. The person Zina confided in and relied upon in times of need was gone. "As I rose in the tennis world there was more and more pressure on me," Zina explains. "My mother was the one I would go to for help and understanding. After my mother died it felt as if there was a hole inside of me. I used food to comfort me and to fill that hole."

Living in hotel rooms—as her life on tour forced her to do—Zina relied on room service to deliver large quantities of food. She would stuff herself with pizza, potato chips, cold cereal, and chocolate. She ate until she could hold no more. "I ate until I made myself sick," she says. "Then I would go to the bathroom and stick my finger down my throat and throw up. I also took diuretics to force my body to rid itself of the food. No one knew I was doing this, but by the time I was twenty-one I was a full-fledged bulimic."

According to estimates by the National Association of Anorexia Nervosa and Related Disorders (ANAD) , eating disorders have reached epidemic levels in the United States. Approximately seven million women and one million men suffer from anorexia, bulimia, and binge-eating problems. Recent studies by ANAD show that one in eleven high-school-age students are afflicted with eating disorders. Typically, people with anorexia are obsessed with the fear of gaining weight and so they starve themselves by continuous dieting or compulsive exercise. People afflicted with bulimia think about food nearly all the time, eating large amounts in secret and then vomiting or purging the body by overusing laxatives, diuretics, or diet pills. Binge eaters devour great amounts of food in one sitting and usually gain weight rapidly.

Nancy Clark, a nutritionist and author of *The*

Sports Nutrition Handbook, says, "The images we see in movies, television, and magazines are that a very thin body is the perfect body. Many eating disorders are caused by females trying to attain a certain image of what they think is perfect. Bodies come in all sizes and weights. Girls and women, in particular, need to know that they are perfect just the way they are. It is so important to love and accept yourself regardless of how your body looks."

Because she was always big for her age, with a muscular lower body, Zina found it difficult to accept the way she looked. "I had to wear those skimpy little tennis outfits which never fit my particular body," she says. "I was always self-conscious of how I looked. It did not help when I heard people saying, 'Oooh, her thighs are like Earl Campbell's [a rugged Houston Oilers fullback].' When I was young I was constantly trying to meet someone else's standards of who I should be. I didn't realize it was OK to be myself."

In addition to her dissatisfaction with the way she looked and the void left by the loss of her mother, Zina was also crushed by the burden of expectations placed on her by other black people. When she beat Chris Evert for the first time in 1985 her life changed dramatically in this respect. "Everyone in the African-American community was now counting on me to do well," she says. "Being the next great African-American player was extremely stressful and, looking back on it, I did not deal with it well."

When the pressures of her life closed in on her, Zina resorted to binge-eating and then purging her body of the foods. After five or six years of this, she began to lose her confidence on the court and to run out of energy in the middle of matches. Because she was purging the food from her body before it was fully digested, her system did not have the chance to acquire the nutrients it needed to maintain strength and energy.

Zina hit rock bottom at a tournament in Kansas City when she lost to the 300th-ranked player in the world. Alone in her room that night, after six years of suffering in secret, she happened to turn on the television and see a commercial that described the problems of people with eating disorders. She watched intently and realized that she, too, had a problem that was out of hand. It was time to ask for help.

For three months she placed her tennis career on hold while she received therapy from a counselor who specialized in eating disorders. "I came to see how I used food to ease the pains of life," she explains. "It was time to face up to the loss of my mother and to start dealing with the pressures in my life in different ways. I was a perfectionist, always striving to be better. I had to learn to love myself as I am, and to stop trying to be someone else or to look like someone I am not."

These were hard lessons for Zina to learn, but she slowly gained control of her problems and her tennis career. In 1988 she represented the United States in the Summer Olympic Games in Seoul, Korea. She brought home a bronze medal for her play in singles competition. At the prestigious Wimbledon event in 1991, Zina stunned French Open champion Monica Seles, breaking her thirty-eight-match win streak, to set up a battle against defending Wimbledon champ Steffi Graf in the semifinals. From the outset of the match with Graf, Zina pounced on her opponent's forehands and drilled them back over the net. Zina danced across the court from one baseline to the other, returning everything as if she could read where Graf would place the ball. At match point, as she had done all day, Zina outsmarted her opponent. With Graf prepared for a wide forehand serve, Zina cranked up a bullet serve that zipped into the corner of the service box on the backhand side. Graf stood in stunned silence as the announcer called out: "Game, set, and match to Miss Garrison."

Two days later Zina found herself living the dream of every tennis player, amateur and professional: She stood on Centre Court for the finals at Wimbledon. Unfortunately she stood across from the greatest women's tennis player of all time, Martina Navratilova. Early in the match Zina slammed a forehand winner past Navratilova, but Martina calmly dug the shot out of the grass and returned it with a beautiful backhand stroke. That great return set the tone for the entire match. A moment later Navratilova

Zina Garrison

commanded the lead and never looked back, defeating Zina and claiming an unprecedented ninth Wimbledon title. Despite the loss, playing in the finals was a thrilling moment in Zina's long and successful career. She retired in 1997, having won more than five hundred matches, which places her in a select group of tennis superstars.

Although she still suffers an occasional relapse, Zina has gained control over her eating disorder. She thinks about why she feels so driven to eat and tries to deal with her feelings by examining them honestly rather than by eating. She has developed a network of family and friends whom she can call to discuss her feelings, instead of burying the feelings with food.

"Bulimia is a difficult condition to suffer with," she says, "because you must have food in order to live. An alcoholic can avoid alcohol once he realizes it is a problem, but a bulimic cannot avoid food. I have learned that hiding your problems is one of the worst things you can do. Whatever the problem, find someone to confide in and talk about it."

In her hometown of Houston, Zina is well known for helping children. She joined Kid Care of Houston to help supply children with hot meals. She also created the Zina Garrison All-Court Tennis Academy, which offers inner-city children the chance to learn tennis and to build self esteem. Zina often works at the academy, serving as an instructor and friend to many children. She listens to children and helps them with their problems, offering advice when it is needed.

"With eating disorders, as with any problem," she says, "the best thing you can do is talk with someone. It's painful to admit you have a problem, but we all have problems. There is no shame in asking for help when you need it. Above all else, remember that you must love yourself regardless of what others are saying."

Bob Welch
Living One Day at a Time

It is October 11, 1978. The New York Yankees trail the Los Angeles Dodgers, 4-3, in the ninth inning of the second game of the World Series. Two New York runners dance off base as Reggie Jackson strides to the plate. The Yankee outfielder, nicknamed "Mr. October" for his clutch postseason hitting, has already knocked in all three runs for his team. The future Hall of Fame slugger glares menacingly at the mound where a raw, unknown rookie named Bob Welch peers in at the catcher. In a duel of power versus power, Welch proceeds to fire 95-mile-per-hour fastballs to the dangerous hitter.

The first pitch blows past Jackson's mighty swing for strike one. The slugger's grunts can be heard in the stands behind home plate, but Welch does not flinch. The two players are locked in a nine-pitch, seven-minute duel that baseball historians will later call one of the greatest baseball dramas of all time. With the count full at three balls and two strikes, the runners break for the next base. Welch delivers a laserlike fastball and Jackson's body twists into a mammoth swing that corkscrews him around, thrusting him forward, left knee touching the ground. The umpire shouts, "Strike three!" and young Bob Welch pumps his arm in the air as teammates mob him on the mound.

For one brief moment in time he is Bob Welch, World Series hero.

Welch's teammates can hardly believe that this starry-eyed newcomer has saved the game. Just a few months before he was pitching in the minor leagues and now he walks among them, one of the guys. More than one Dodger lifts a glass to toast the man who shut down Mr. October. And Bob Welch is more than happy to lift his own glass in return.

Although Reggie Jackson and the Yankees went on to get the best of both Welch and the Dodgers, Bob's friends in Ferndale, Michigan, were eager to buy him drinks all that winter. It was party time for a star on the rise, but in just two years Bob's heavy drinking would send his star crashing back to earth. By spring training of his third year he would stand before his teammates and announce: "I am an alcoholic. I always will be an alcoholic."

"I grew up in a hard-working, hard-drinking town outside of Detroit," Bob says. "It was part of everyday life to meet at the bar after work and drink for hours. It was inevitable that I would drink growing up. A bunch of guys I knew were doing it and I wanted to see what it was like. Some guys didn't like it, but everyone tried it. I liked it. I just couldn't control it."

Bob's first taste of alcohol came when he was ten. At his sister's wedding Bob and his cousin sidled up to the drink table. When no one was looking they sneaked mixed drinks off the table and gulped them down. At fifteen Bob and his friends illegally bought cheap wine and chugged it down on the way to a football game. It was the cool thing to do in his town and Bob wanted to be one of the guys, so he did it, too. In high school Bob drank mostly on weekends, but sometimes, when he was a senior, he would leave school at midday and stop for lunch and beer with friends.

Several things about his personality seemed to draw Bob to alcohol. From a very early age, he had a great deal of nervous energy but was shy around people. "Drinking seemed to make everything easier," he says. "I would get a buzz on and stop being afraid of girls. I wanted to hide from the feelings I had, like being nervous and being afraid of not being liked. For a few hours drinking helped me forget my troubles."

Of course, when Bob awoke the next morning the troubles he tried to hide from were still there, but it took him years to realize that alcohol was just a temporary escape. By the time he was a high school senior Bob had developed into a top-notch pitcher and a steady drinker. He attended Eastern Michigan University and began to drink even more heavily, although it did not seem to affect his play on the baseball field. Coaches and scouts across the country began to notice Bob's prowess on the pitching mound, and he was chosen to be on a college all-star team that would tour Japan.

In Japan he was removed early from one of the games. In an angry mood he sneaked off and stole some cases of beer. In short order he guzzled much of the beer, opened his fifth-floor hotel window, strolled out on the balcony, and began walking along a twelve-inch ledge. When he returned inside he kicked down a door. Later, teammates had to describe his bizarre behavior to him because Bob had been so drunk that he could recall nothing. Word of his excessive drinking made its way back to the United States and his college coach, but Bob did not view any of this as a problem.

Throughout college, alcohol played a more important part in Bob's world. When he went out to dinner with his longtime girlfriend (and future wife) Mary Ellen, his attention was on the bottle, not on her. "We would order wine and I'd drink most of it," he says. "I thought I was having a great time, but I couldn't remember the taste of the food or what we talked about. What I really cared about was draining my glass as fast as possible."

In 1977 the Dodgers selected Bob in the first round of the free agent draft. He reported to the Dodgers AA minor league team, and soon realized that professional baseball provided many opportunities to drink. As a starting pitcher he only worked every fourth or fifth day, which meant he could drink two or three days in a row before having to prepare to pitch. And he often did just that.

In a book he wrote with George Vecsey, *Five O'Clock Comes Early: A Young Man's Battle With Alcoholism,* Bob tells how easy it was to support a drinking addiction while playing baseball. "There was beer in the clubhouse and a couple of bars in every hotel. An alcoholic can find a drink in the middle of Death Valley. I know I could."

Sometimes Bob would drink all night. Sometimes he would start in the afternoon and stop when he could no longer stand up. Because it did not seem to affect his pitching, few people commented on his behavior. Bob would angrily deny that he had a problem to anyone who did mention his drinking.

Although Bob started the 1978 season in the minors, the Dodgers called him up to the Major League team in June. He was an important contributor to the Dodgers' run for the pennant and, despite the World Series loss to the Yankees, he became a hero to Dodgers fans. But a winter spent partying led to a 1979 season of heavier drinking. Teammates caught him sneaking alcohol into his hotel in a brown paper bag. During games he would wander into the clubhouse and drink beer when no one was looking. One day in San Francisco he drank so much before the game that he fell face-first in the outfield during warmups. He later picked a fight with one of the Giants outfielders.

Another time, after drinking beer with buddies, Bob tried to impress them with some driving tricks in his Bronco on the beach. The Bronco flipped over and the three drinking buddies narrowly avoided serious injury. It was clear to some in the Dodgers clubhouse that Bob Welch was allowing alcohol to destroy his career and his life.

Several members of the Dodgers organization talked with Bob and persuaded him to attend sessions at a rehabilitation facility in Arizona known as The Meadows. At first he continued to deny he even had a problem. *After all,* he thought, *I don't look anything like the puffy-faced, wrinkly old drunks and drug addicts who are in this program.* He was told by his counselors over and over again that the first step toward helping yourself is to admit that you have a problem. "When you admit to yourself that you are and always will be an alcoholic, then you've got a start," Bob explains. "I came to see that I have no control over alcohol. The fact is, I'm crazy when I drink. If I had continued to drink, I would probably have been killed in a car accident by now."

According to Dr. Robert A. Zucker, the director of the University of Michigan Alcohol Research Center, "People don't regard it as such, but alcohol is a drug. It can be very addictive and dangerous because it is part of the lifestyle of most societies. It is all around us—at parties, at weddings, and even at funerals. For some people it is impossible to say no once they get started drinking."

A 1996 study by the National Council on Alcoholism and Drug Dependence brought to light the fact that an alarming number of drinkers are children. About nine million Americans aged twelve to twenty were current drinkers, consuming anywhere from an occasional drink to many drinks every month. Of these young drinkers, 1.9 million were considered heavy drinkers.

"Adolescence is a time when young people are more likely to take risks without being aware of the dangerous consequences," Dr. Zucker says. "Alcohol is a drug which can lead to troublesome behavior."

While he was at The Meadows, Bob Welch came to understand how he started using alcohol as a teenager to bury his problems and feelings. "I learned to be more honest with my feelings and my relationships with people. I learned to recognize my feelings and deal with them—without alcohol. When you drink to bury your feelings you are only deceiving yourself. After the alcohol wears off, your problems are still there waiting for you."

Upon completing alcohol rehabilitation, Bob showed up at spring training in 1980 and made a startling admission to his teammates. "I'm an alcoholic," he stated, "but now I know how to stop drinking, one day at a time, and that is what I am going to do."

True to his word, Bob has not picked up another drink in more than twenty years. He resumed his baseball career and proved to be one of the best pitchers of his era, winning more than one hundred games in both the American and National Leagues. In 1990 he won twenty-seven games for the Oakland Athletics and earned the Cy Young Award as the best pitcher in his league. Although there were times when frustration caused him to think about drinking again, he knew that his body had no tolerance for alcohol. Instead he would force himself to face his frustrations and find a more constructive way to deal with them, such as training harder or trying to figure out what he did wrong on the pitching mound.

"There will always be some kind of temptation for kids," Bob says. "I remember how tough peer pressure was for me. You have to think before you act, and make good decisions. Be aware when you make the wrong decisions and learn from the experience. The tests are there all the time."

Although he has remained sober for twenty years, Bob still attends Alcoholics Anonymous meetings twice a month. He stands before the assembled group and announces: "I'm Bob Welch. I'm an alcoholic but today I'm sober." His plan is to stay that way, living his life one day at a time.

Willie O'Ree
Breaking the Barriers

As he strapped on his hockey skates in the locker room, Willie O'Ree could barely contain his excitement. It was January 18, 1958, and Willie was wearing the black-and-gold jersey of the Boston Bruins. There were only about one hundred players among the National Hockey League's six teams, and Willie O'Ree was now one of them. Few of the fans in attendance at the Montreal Forum realized they were watching history in the making. Not only was this Willie's first game in the NHL, it was also the first time a black player had played in the previously all-white league.

When the coach tapped Willie on the shoulder, he popped off the bench and hopped the gate onto the ice. In a split second he was chasing down the puck and fending off two Montreal Canadiens who came at him with sticks raised high. He dodged the first and flew by the second defender as the crowd's roar echoed in his ears.

Like Jackie Robinson in baseball, Willie O'Ree broke the color barrier in professional hockey. He was a ground-breaker, but he hardly thought so at the time. "I was aware I was the first," O'Ree recalls, "but for me the real thrill was just playing the game."

After all, for Willie the game was always the thing. Growing up in Fredricton, New Brunswick, it seemed that everyone played hockey on the frozen rivers and ponds. Willie's dad built a rink in the backyard, and by age three little Willie was pushing a chair around the ice to help him balance on his double-runner skates. He skated nearly every day and, like many of his friends, began playing in organized hockey leagues as a young boy. "I would play anywhere, at any time, with anyone," Willie says.

The O'Rees were the only black family in the city of Fredricton and all of Willie's friends were white. He starred in rugby, football, baseball, and hockey, and was taunted by opponents in every sport he played. "I knew from school and sports that I had to put up with a certain amount of prejudice," he says. "Players on other teams came after me with high sticks and head shots, but I was determined not to let anyone run me out of the rink or off the field."

Willie's friends and family advised him to ignore the name-calling and cheap shots so many opponents directed his way, and that is just what he did. When players taunted him, Willie gritted his teeth and played a bit harder. As a black player in a mostly white sport Willie knew he would be a target for the hatred that some people carry within them. His older brother Richard practiced with him and taught him valuable lessons on the ice. "One day when we were playing Richard drove me hard into the boards," Willie remembers. "It brought tears to my eyes and I said, 'Why did you do that?' He said, 'If you want to be a pro you will be hit much harder than this. You have to learn to take it and stand up for yourself.'"

As a teenager Willie's baseball skills were so good that the Milwaukee Braves invited him to training camp in the spring of 1956. Coming from a small Canadian town to Atlanta, Georgia, for training camp was an eye-opening experience. In the airport, Willie saw restroom signs that said "Whites Only" and "Colored Only." He was made to sit in the back of the bus wherever he traveled in the South. There were restaurants that refused to serve black people, and hotels where he was told his kind was not welcome. On an outing after church one Sunday, Willie and a few Latin and black teammates were waiting to be served in a small-town drugstore when several white customers threatened to harm them, forcing them to leave in a hurry.

On the bus ride back to Canada after his tryout, Willie considered his options in baseball. "To be honest," he says now, "I don't know if I could have concentrated on baseball with all that prejudice. As we drove through the South I was praying to God to help me stay safe and get back home."

With his blazing speed and skating ability, Willie did not need baseball. He turned his full attention to hockey and moved through the ranks of the amateur and semi-professional leagues. When he was 18, during his second year of junior hockey in Kitchener, Ontario, Willie was skating up the ice when he was struck in the face by the puck. Like other players of his day, Willie did not wear a face guard or helmet to deflect the puck, and the impact broke his nose and part of his jaw, and severely damaged his right eye. His retina was injured so badly that he lost nearly all the vision in the eye, and he was warned by his parents and doctors to give up the fast-paced sport.

After an eight-week recovery period Willie was at a career crossroad. "I thought, what will I do if I can't play hockey?" he says. "I told myself, you've still got one good eye so I guess you can play." Shortly after that Willie signed a professional contract with the Quebec Aces of the Quebec League, just one step below the NHL.

At the time there were a number of black players starring in semi-professional hockey across Canada. Stan Maxwell was a talented black center who played with Willie for eight years. "We played a lot of exhibition games against NHL teams and we always fared pretty well," Maxwell says. "There were black players who had the skills to make it in the NHL, but they never got the call. It wasn't easy to be the first black called up, but Willie had the character and dignity to do well with it."

Hockey historian Stan Fischler describes the NHL of the 1950s in this way: "As in society itself there was a significant amount of prejudice in hockey at that time. Back then every player in the NHL was from Canada and there were very few blacks living in Canada playing hockey. But yes, there were certainly some black players who deserved more of a chance. Willie O'Ree was brought up to the Bruins because they needed good players and he was good."

When he was called up by the Boston Bruins in 1958, Willie realized it was only to fill in for an injured player. After two games he was sent back to continue his career in the small cities and dimly lit rinks of the semipro leagues. In 1959 Willie played in the Eastern League, but he returned to the Bruins for forty-three games in the 1960-61 season. He tells the story of his first NHL goal with delight. "It was on New Year's Day and it was against the Montreal Canadiens. It was the second period and I was at left wing. I broke down the side, took a pass, skated around two defensemen, dropped my shoulder, made some moves, and shot. It hit the left goal post and went in."

Willie's goal was the game winner and drew a two-minute standing ovation from the crowd.

His NHL career lasted forty-five games in which he scored four goals and assisted on ten others. Although the reason was never revealed to him, Willie suspects that his NHL career was cut short when word got out about his eye injury. There was a league rule preventing players with serious eye injuries from performing. The Bruins traded him to Montreal who then sent him to the Los Angeles Blades of the Western Hockey League. After six years in L.A., Willie played another seven years with the San Diego Gulls.

In all, Willie played twenty-one seasons of professional hockey, experiencing both the best and worst of human behavior. In each city he played, Willie developed strong friendships with teammates both black and white. In some arenas though, he was spit on and called ugly names, and had things thrown at him.

Perhaps the ugliest incident took place in Chicago where an opponent nailed him with the butt end of his stick, knocking out Willie's front teeth. A fight ensued and Willie needed a police escort out of the arena to guarantee his safety. "I never wanted to fight," Willie says, "but some players wanted to see what you were made of and that was the only way to gain their respect. My parents brought me up to be proud of who I am. You can't change the color of your skin, nor would I want to. But you can change the outlook people have toward you by hard work and by representing yourself in a good manner."

In his job with the NHL's Hockey Diversity Task Force, Willie travels around providing equipment, encouragement, and the benefit of his experience to minority children hoping to play hockey. "There is no substitute for hard work," he tells the young players at his hockey clinics. "Do well in school, set goals for yourself, and most important of all, be proud of who you are."

He may have been the first black hockey player in the NHL, but black stars like Mike Crier and Grant Fuhr are proof that Willie O'Ree will not be the last.

Dan O'Brien
No Sure Thing

The 1992 U.S. Olympic Trials are well underway on this sweltering New Orleans day. Sprinters, jumpers, and long distance runners mill around the track, awaiting their turn to compete, all sharing a similar dream. Each athlete hopes to perform well enough to make the U.S. Olympic team and to bring home a medal. But there is rarely a sure thing in these trials, and most will fall short of their goals and return home disappointed.

Dan O'Brien is the closest to a sure thing at the trials. He is at the top of his game, the reigning world champion in the decathlon. For several weeks now television advertisements have trumpeted his arrival as the nation's next sports superstar. Although it is a month before the Olympics begin, nearly everyone expects that Dan will win the trials, grab the Olympic gold medal, and set a new world record.

The pressure to win is intense as Dan stands at the edge of the pole-vault runway, staring straight ahead. It is the second day of competition in the decathlon, and he leads the field by an almost insurmountable margin. The pole vault is the eighth of ten events, but due to a stress fracture in his right leg Dan has not practiced it much in the past few months. The bar is set at 15 feet, 9 inches, a height he has cleared hundreds of times in practice. He eyes the bar and launches into the first of three attempts to clear it. Dan sprints down the runway, plants the long pole, and flips awkwardly, soaring well below the bar. On his second attempt he sails high in the air, but crashes down onto the bar, sending it bouncing off the standard and to the ground. As he dusts himself off Dan thinks, "This should not be happening to me. Somebody, do something!"

Although his coaches try to calm him, Dan is on his own. If he doesn't clear the bar on this final attempt he will receive no score for the pole vault and will plummet from the lead to twelfth place. With only two events remaining, Dan will not have time to recover. He will not make the Olympic team if he does not make this vault.

"You've done this hundreds of times," he reminds himself before sprinting down the runway. With a final kick Dan plants the 15-foot pole and swings upward toward the bar. For an instant, he seems to hang suspended. Then suddenly he drops, short of the bar, short of his dreams.

"Dan O'Brien, sure thing," said the reporters and

track analysts before he crash-landed at the Olympic Trials. Now they were saying that the only sure thing about him was that he was a loser who choked under pressure. Although he finished strong in the last two events, Dan was out of the running and did not make the Olympic team. It was a crushing blow, but Dan had battled hard times and failure all his life, so this was nothing new.

Right from the start Dan's life was marked by hardship. Shortly after he was born, Dan's parents—an African-American man and a white woman—gave him up for adoption. After two years in various foster homes Dan was adopted by Jim and Virginia O'Brien of Klamath Falls, Oregon. The O'Briens provided a loving and lively family life, and Dan shared farm chores with his seven siblings, six of whom were adopted.

Although his family was large and included a Cherokee, a Korean, and a Hispanic sibling, Dan was the only African-American. "The hardest part was that no one in my family looked like me," he says. "I was the only one in my entire area who even faintly resembled a black person. The only knowledge I had about being black I took from the sitcoms on television."

Although his biracial background made Dan one-of-a-kind at school, he was popular because he was funny and a talented athlete. Early in his school career, though, Dan experienced his first real taste of failure.

Living on a farm he had lots of space to roam, and after chores were done Dan would go fishing, ride his bicycle, or shoot baskets. As long as his body was moving he was happy. But the rules were different in school. He was asked to sit quietly and to listen for hours on end, and he could not do it.

"I couldn't focus on what I was reading for even twenty minutes," Dan says. "I couldn't remember what I'd just read. I could never sit still, so I became the class clown. I was always behind in my work." On more than one occasion Dan's parents considered holding him back in school, but they decided against it and he managed to scrape by one year at a time.

By the time Dan entered high school his athletic skills were blossoming. As a junior he was the leading scorer and rebounder on the basketball team. In football he was an all-state wide receiver and kicker. At the state track meet Dan won the 100-meter dash, 110-meter hurdles, 300-meter hurdles, and the long jump, single-handedly outscoring every other team.

When he was running, jumping, or throwing, Dan was content. At home, however, his parents enforced a strict rule that tied together school and sports: If your grade in any subject was lower than a C average you could not participate in sports. "One semester I received a D in Social Studies," Dan remembers. "It was heartbreaking to walk past track practice one day and know that I could not participate."

Encouraged by the assistant track coach his freshman year of high school, Dan first tried the ten-event decathlon in 1981. By the time his high school career was over he was the national junior champion in the event, and he was offered an athletic scholarship to the University of Idaho. When he arrived at college Dan was completely unprepared for the amount of studying he would have to do to succeed. As a student he was disorganized and could not focus on his work. In a number of courses Dan received F's or incompletes because his work wasn't handed in on time. He hung out with a crowd of party-goers and began to spend more time at parties than he did in the classroom.

At the end of his junior year in college Dan flunked out and lost his scholarship. "I wasn't giving school any effort, and because of that I felt like a loser," he says. "I sat in the stands watching the track team practice and slid out unnoticed, feeling terrible. I was in debt and ashamed to go home. Finally I had a good, hard look at myself and said, 'This has got to stop.'"

Dan enrolled in a two-year community college, where he came to grips with the fact that he had wasted three years of a college education and, because of bad grades, had not competed even once in a track-and-field meet. He learned to organize his notes and to concentrate on studying instead of partying. Several years later, when Dan was twenty-five, he discovered the reason he had had so much trouble concentrating in school. Dan suffers with Attention Deficit Hyperactivity Disorder (ADHD). This made it difficult for him to sit and focus for any length of time without feeling the need to jump up and move around. To overcome ADHD Dan needed to work for short periods of time, take plenty of study breaks, and continually review and repeat what he had just studied.

At Spokane Community College Dan picked his grades up and learned the importance of education. "I realized I was wasting my abilities and my opportunities," he says. Dan's improved grades allowed him to re-enroll at Idaho and to compete in track his senior year. Most track athletes only have to master one or two events, but in a two-day period a decathlete must compete in ten events: the 100- and 400-meter runs, 110-meter hurdles, long jump and high jump, javelin, discus, shot put, pole vault, and, finally, the 1500-meter run. It is a tremendous test of strength, speed, and endurance, but Dan proved he was up to the task during his senior year at Idaho. That year he was named the Big Sky Conference Indoor Track and Field Athlete of the Year.

After graduating from Idaho, Dan often spent six or more hours training each day. In 1990 he made people take notice when he scored 8,483 points in a decathlon. And in 1991 he won the decathlon title at the World Track and Field Championships, establishing himself as the favorite for the next year's Olympic Games.

But when Dan failed to clear the pole-vault bar at the Olympic Trials in New Orleans, he was crushed. "I felt left out," he says. "Not making the Olympic team felt like it did in elementary school when I didn't get picked for a team. Man, it hurt. It was very hard to get over for a couple of weeks." When he returned home to Moscow, Idaho, however, scores of phone messages awaited him on his answering machine. Each message encouraged Dan to hold his head high and not abandon his dreams. For the next two weeks, Dan hung out with friends and healed his wounded spirit.

Dan accepted a job as a broadcaster and flew to Barcelona, Spain, to watch and comment on the 1992 Olympic Games. He soon found himself inspired by the courageous performances of the greatest athletes in the world.

"I realized then that sometimes bad things happen to good people," Dan points out. "But you cannot give up. You have to move on to your next goal. You have to learn from your failures because sports are a process, like life. You have to be ready to fail and to take the ups and downs in stride."

When the Olympics were over Dan resumed training with a vengeance. As a decathlete he realized that he could not win every event, so it was important to improve his performance in his weaker events while making sure not to torment himself with thoughts of past failures. According to his coach, Rick Sloan, "The real healing begins when you get back out and try again, when you take the first step toward your next goal. Likc any great decathlete, Dan's strength is his ability to forget about his failures and to take it one step at a time."

One month after the 1992 Olympics, Dan broke the world decathlon record at a meet in Talence, France. Over the next four years he won two world championships and was the top-ranked decathlete in the world each year.

"Every time I was in the pole vault, that failure in New Orleans was on my mind," he admits. "I was angry about failing, but I used that as motivation. 'That's never going to happen to me again,' I told myself." Dan concentrated on the pole vault and at the 1996 Olympic Trials he easily cleared the bar at 17 feet, 3/4 inch. That helped him earn a spot on the U.S. Olympic team.

Six years before the 1996 Olympic Games in Atlanta, Georgia, Dan had written his goal on a scrap of paper. It said: "World's Greatest Athlete." By Dan's reckoning, a gold medal in Atlanta would set the record straight and confirm that he was the best in the world. On the first day of competition Dan won the opening and closing events to quickly lead the field. He handled the pole vault with ease on the second day, and held a commanding lead by the time he lined up for the last event, the 1500-meter run. As he crossed the finish line, breaking the Olympic decathlon record, gold medalist O'Brien blew kisses to the sky, fell down on one knee, and cried. Now he could throw away that little scrap of paper because there was no longer any doubt: Dan O'Brien was the greatest athlete in the world.

Jean Driscoll

Don't Look Back

Like the pistons of a race-car engine, Jean Driscoll's arms pump up and down, pulling her forward at sixteen miles per hour. Though she has won the women's wheelchair division of the Boston Marathon each of the past six years, she now lags behind three rivals. Fueled by their own dreams of victory, the competition is out to prove that Driscoll is no longer queen of the hill. But Jean has spent a lifetime proving others wrong, and the 1996 marathon would be no different.

In the middle of a steep hill Jean muscles into overdrive and passes her bewildered opponents. On the way down she is a blur, reaching speeds of nearly fifty miles per hour. She never looks back. A crowd of thousands shouts her name as she breaks the tape to claim a seventh straight victory in the most famous road race in the world. At twenty-nine she is the superstar of her sport; a world-class athlete like Jackie Joyner-Kersee or Michael Jordan. Not bad for a kid doctors predicted would never amount to much.

Jean Driscoll was born with spina bifida, a hole in the lower portion of her backbone that affected her leg muscles and bathroom functions. The doctors warned her parents that she would never walk, go to a regular school, or live independently as an adult. At best, they cautioned, she would have a sit-down job in which she relied on her hands, like a secretary.

"From age two on I adopted an 'I'll prove you wrong' attitude," Jean says. "My siblings and parents never allowed me to act disabled, and I was determined to be like all the kids in the neighborhood."

With the help of below-the-knee braces, Jean learned to walk when she was two. Since her parents worked long hours, Jean and her four siblings were required to pitch in with household chores. It may have taken her longer, but Jean could lug the laundry basket up from the basement, one step at a time, just like her older sister. And, like the others, she was expected to make her bed, wash the dishes, and vacuum, too.

Jean attended the same elementary school in Milwaukee as her brothers and sister. In good weather she walked down the block to school; when the sidewalks were coated with ice and snow she was pulled in a little red wagon by a family member. "My siblings would fight over who would pull me," Jean says. "I always felt like a burden. Sometimes they would forget to bring me home and I'd wait at school for an hour, knowing they were eating snacks and watching cartoons. It was so frustrating to be able to see my house but not be able to get there. And it was humiliating to be an eighth grader being pulled to school by your little brother."

At school Jean tried to focus on how similar she was to her classmates. She did not understand how a little hole in her spine could make her so different. Because of that hole Jean could not always control her bathroom functions. She kept a bag with extra underwear available, but by fourth grade bathroom accidents were a major embarrassment. "I was constantly mad at God," she explains. "Why did you make me have spina bifida, I would ask."

As a girl Jean loved sports and was eager to join neighborhood races and games. Her leg braces allowed her to walk awkwardly, swaying side to side and dragging her feet. She could not keep up with her friends, though, so she settled for jobs like scorekeeper or manager.

Despite warnings from her doctors that walking placed unnecessary pressure on her hips, Jean refused to give up activities that other kids performed routinely. When she watched friends racing around the block on fancy ten-speed bikes, she was determined to ditch her babyish one-speed with training wheels. One Saturday when she was nine years old, Jean went to a friend's house and borrowed her little brother's two-wheeler.

She practiced all day until she could master the pedals, the steering, and the art of balancing. With great pride she raced home to show her mother, who promptly screamed, "You're going to break your neck!"

But it was a hip, not her neck, that proved to be Jean's downfall. After bike-riding without any problems for several years, at age fourteen Jean crashed when she cut a corner too hard. The pedal dug into the cement and Jean slammed down on her left hip, badly dislocating it. When she was operated on, the surgeons discovered that Jean's hips were badly worn down. Over the course of the next year Jean required five operations to deepen her hip sockets and transfer muscles to strengthen the area. During her recovery she lay in a full-body cast on a hospital bed in the family living room. "It was a helpless state to be in," Jean sadly recounts. "I had to depend on everyone for everything, but I could tolerate it if it meant that I would walk again."

Just two weeks after her body cast was removed, Jean's left hip dislocated again. Nothing more could be done, her doctors told her. She would have to throw away the leg braces and learn to handle a wheelchair. Her days of walking were over, and Jean was devastated. "I hated my body and my disability. I felt I was less of a person in a wheelchair," Jean says. "I wasn't prepared for this. It took years and years to get a grip on what it meant to use a wheelchair."

The thought of being permanently dependent on

others was repulsive to Jean. At the mall and in school people stared at her in her wheelchair, making her more self-conscious and ashamed of her body. Her sister would break the tension by calling out to those who stared, "Take a picture, it'll last longer."

Throughout high school Jean struggled to accept life in a wheelchair. There were other teenagers in school who used wheelchairs, but she never considered herself one of them. Finally, a boy she knew who also had spina bifida spent months convincing her to attend a wheelchair soccer game. What she saw opened her eyes. "When the game started, chairs were crashing and bodies were flying," she says with a giggle. "If players flipped out of their chairs, no one was horrified, babied, or patronized. I thought, 'Now *this* is sports.'" Jean joined the game and slowly began to change her views on having a disability. Nevertheless, the road to accepting herself was lined with potholes and she seemed destined to hit every one.

After high school Jean enrolled in a nursing program in Milwaukee. Although she had been a strong student in high school, she could not concentrate on her studies and flunked out after three semesters. At the same time, Jean developed pressure sores from sitting for hours at a time with no muscle or padding to cushion her skin from her bones. She was hospitalized three times to heal the dangerous and painful sores. On top of this, she suddenly learned that her parents had decided to get a divorce. After a childhood filled with physical pain and mental anguish, at nineteen Jean's spirit could sink no lower. "I thought the world would be a better place without me," Jean admits. "I had suicidal thoughts. I had to learn to like and respect myself. That was the number one thing."

A nurse who knew Jean hired her to work as a nanny for her two young children. Before long Jean realized she could place the children on her lap and use her wheelchair to "take a walk" to the park so they could play. Jean had been confined by the chair and its limitations for four years, but she began to realize that it also provided a freedom of movement. Now she was ready to try wheelchair tennis and soccer. The more she played the more she realized that sports helped her come to terms with her problems. It felt so good to be active that she played a lot.

While playing wheelchair soccer she met University of Illinois wheelchair coach Brad Hedrick. He was so impressed by Jean's speed and strength that he recruited her to attend the school and play for its basketball team. For the first time in her life she met people in wheelchairs who did not define themselves solely by their disabilities. They worked at regular jobs, were happily married, and were living productive lives. "My entire life my disability had been my excuse," Jean says. "I thought it was the reason I couldn't do the things my friends could, like playing sports or having certain boyfriends. I came to realize a disability is just a characteristic, like being born nearsighted. A nearsighted person wakes up in the morning and puts on glasses, never giving his vision problem a second thought all day. My wheelchair is the first thing I see each morning. I get in and don't give it another thought all day."

With a full slate of courses in speech communication and several hours of sports each day, Jean had no time for self-pity. She set goals for herself and became a different person. Her racing career began when friends convinced her to enter an eight-kilometer event using her regular wheelchair. Though she finished well behind the leaders, the race sparked her interest.

Soon she was training with the university's legendary wheelchair track coach, Marty Morse. Under Morse's guidance Jean built her body into a finely tuned racing machine. In a 26.2-mile marathon race she would need to stroke the wheels at least six thousand times. To do so with the force necessary to win would require the muscle power capable of handling six thousand push-ups. So Jean hit the weight room.

Years of grueling weight-training sessions empowered her to the point that she could lift 220 pounds over her head—nearly double her body weight. In addition to weight work Jean routinely logged 60 to 120 miles of roadwork weekly on the rural roads near the campus. As her times dropped steadily, her confidence and faith in herself grew. "I began to understand that the biggest limitations are those you place on yourself or allow others to place on you," she says. "I survived the mental torment of my childhood. Now it was time to learn from it."

Using a lightweight racing wheelchair, Jean captured her first national level race in Spokane, Washington, in 1989. Her confidence was sky-high, so she entered her first marathon and placed second in Chicago. In her first Boston Marathon she blew the competition away and broke a course record by out-climbing everyone on the hills. Since 1990 she has dominated her sport, with several world and numerous course records to her name. Jean also grabbed the silver medals in the 800-meter wheelchair event at the 1992 and 1996 Summer Olympic Games.

Jean has jogged three times with President Clinton, appeared on many television shows, and been paid to give inspirational speeches around the world. While maintaining a hectic training, racing, and speaking schedule, Jean has also found time to complete her undergraduate and master's degrees, and to receive an honorary doctorate from the University of Rhode Island.

"Successful people are those who fall off the horse a dozen times and hop back on a dozen times," Jean says. "If you dream big and work hard, you can be one of those people who make it."

It has been quite a ride for Jean Driscoll, but maybe

the doctors were right after all. She *does* earn her living using her hands at a sit-down job: racing a seventeen-pound wheelchair faster than any woman in the world.

Jean Driscoll

INDEX

Abdul-Jabbar, Kareem, 58
Akers, Michelle, 9, 19-26
Alcoholics Anonymous, 62, 116
alcoholism, 53-63, 109-116
American Foundation for the Blind, 16, 18
Arizona State University, 5
Attention Deficit Hyperactivity Disorder, 129

Bahrami, Mansour, 64-72
Barry, Rick, 58
Batura Glacier, 13
Blechman, Mickey, 31
blindness, 10-18
Borg, Bjorn, 70
Boston Bruins, 117, 121-122
Boston College, 13
Boston Marathon, 133, 140
Brosnihan, Diana Golden, 82-89
bulimia nervosa, 99-108

cancer, 82, 87-88
Care To Share, 98
Centers for Disease Control and Prevention, 23
Chastain, Brandi, 19
Chicago Bears, 97-98
chronic fatigue syndrome, 19-26
Clark, Nancy, 102
Clinton, Bill, 140
cocaine, 57-63
Connors, Jimmy, 55, 70, 72
Continental Basketball Association, 61

Dartmouth College, 86
Davis Cup, 55, 66
Devers, Gail, 35-44
diabetes, 92, 101
DiCicco, Tony, 20-21, 24
Driscoll, Jean, 86, 133-141

Eastern Michigan University, 111
eating disorders, 99-108
Eisenreich, Jim 45-52
Epstein-Barr virus, 23
Erving, Julius, 58
Evert, Chris, 99-100

Fignon, Laurent, 78-79
Fischler, Stan, 121
Frazier, Walt, 58
French Open, 69-70, 101

Garrison, Zina, 99-108
Georgetown University, 66
Gerulaitis, Vitas, 55
Gibson, Althea, 100
Golden Gate Gators, 57
Golden State Warriors, 58
Gonzalez, Ruben, 27-34
Graf, Steffi, 105
Graves disease, 35-44

Hedrick, Brad, 138
Hillecher, Jerry, 33
Hockey Diversity Task Force (NHL), 122-123
Hogan, Marty, 33
Houston Rockets, 53, 57-58, 61

Jackson, Reggie, 109-110
Johnson, Magic, 57

Kansas City Royals, 51
Kersee, Bobby, 36, 41
Kid Care of Houston, 107
Koufax, Sandy, 8
Kriek, Johan, 70

LeMond, Greg, 73-81
Lesley College, 14
Los Angeles Blades, 122
Los Angeles Dodgers, 5, 51, 109-110, 112-115
Lucas, John, 53-63

Machu Picchu, 13
Malone, Moses, 58
Mantle, Mickey, 8
Marinovich, Todd, 95
Maxwell, Stan, 120
McEnroe, John, 70
Milwaukee Braves, 119
Minnesota Twins, 47-51
mitochondria myopathy, 79
Montreal Canadiens, 117, 121-122
Morse, Marty, 139
Mt. Kilimanjaro, 15
Mt. McKinley, 10, 15-18
Mt. Rainier, 15-16, 88

National Association of Anorexia Nervosa
and Related Disorders, 102
National Council on Alcoholism and Drug Dependence, 115
Navratilova, Martina, 105, 107
New Jersey Nets, 57
New York Mets, 5-6
New York Yankees, 109-110
Notre Dame, 94-98
Nuveen Tour, 70

Oakland Athletics, 116
O'Brien, Dan, 9, 124-132
Olympic Games, 7-8, 24, 35, 37, 39-44, 76, 85, 105,
124-126, 129-132, 140
Orange Bowl, 97

O'Ree, Willie, 117-123

Pan American Games, 37
Philadelphia 76ers, 62

Quebec Aces, 120

retinoschisis, 11
Robinson, Jackie, 117

San Antonio Spurs, 61-62
San Diego Gulls, 122
Scurry, Briana, 19
Sloan, Rick, 130
spina bifida, 133-141
Spokane Community College, 129
St. Cloud State College, 47

Team High Sights, 16-18
Texas Rangers, 6
Tour de France, 73, 75-76, 78-79
Tourette syndrome, 45-52
Tourette Syndrome Association, 50, 52

UCLA, 36, 38, 41
University of Maryland, 56-57
University of Idaho, 128-129
University of Illinois, 138-139
University of Rhode Island, 140
U.S. Olympic Festival, 37
U.S. Open tennis, 99
U.S. women's soccer team, 19-26

Valentine, Bobby, 5-6
Vecsey, George, 113
Voll, John, 66-67

Washington Bullets, 59
Washington Redskins, 98
Weihenmayer, Erik, 9-18
Welch, Bob, 109-116
Wilkerson, Tim, 72
Wimbledon, 100, 105-107
World Cup, 19-20, 22
World Games for Disabled Athletes, 85
World Series, 52, 109-110, 113
World Track and Field Championships, 129

Yellen, Mike, 28

Zina Garrison All-Court Tennis Academy, 107
Zora Zorich Scholarship Fund, 98
Zorich, Chris, 90-98
Zucker, Robert A., 114-115